# swimming the ECHO

Brian L. Tucker

eLectio Publishing
Little Elm, TX
www.eLectioPublishing.com

*Swimming the Echo*
By Brian L. Tucker


Cover Design by eLectio Publishing.

ISBN-13: 978-1-63213-382-3

Published by eLectio Publishing, LLC
Little Elm, Texas
http://www.eLectioPublishing.com

Printed in the United States of America

5 4 3 2 1 eLP 21 20 19 18 17

The eLectio Publishing creative team is comprised of: Kaitlyn Campbell, Emily Certain, Lori Draft, Court Dudek, Jim Eccles, Sheldon James, and Christine LePorte.

*For Mom and Dad*

"Time just gets away from us."

– Charles Portis,
*True Grit*

# CHAPTER ONE

Cade Rainy tossed his line out into the water and watched it travel quickly past him and his dad.

The fly rod was effortless in Cade's small, adolescent hand. He zipped it to and fro, maneuvering around a big brown trout as he wiped the sweat from his eyes and pushed his blond, almost bleached white, hair out of the way. The water pummeled the landing just from where the fish, and Cade, danced. Cade's father laughed at the spectacle. Cade set the hook with his lean muscles and waited, watching the fish initiate the fight.

"Turn him! Turn him!" Haven Rainy shouted, running out into the water with his thin waders, splashing Cade as he hugged him.

"I'm trying to fish," Cade said, biting his bottom lip, face pinched in consternation, his dad's gray beard scratching his smooth skin.

"All right. He's yours. Just don't let too much of that line get out of sight . . . as fast as this current's moving, you won't have a fish in a minute. He'll be drowned."

"Fish don't drown," Cade retorted. "And when was the last time I lost a trout?"

Haven looked back to the bank, and Cade followed his gaze. A blue heron had perched on their uncovered bacon and cheese biscuits, nibbling frantically.

"Shhheewww!" Haven yelled, splashing back to shore. "Git, bird! That's ours!"

Cade felt a tug and realized the trout was oblivious to him, and his need to catch it.

"I can't let you get downstream. Someone else might get you. You're too pretty to let loose."

As if understanding him, the fish relented in his escape. He turned sideways and came to the surface, fish belly showing. He wasn't huge, but Cade knew they could add him to their partially-full, five-gallon bucket. Maybe it would amount to enough for dinner.

On the shore, Cade placed his brown trout into the bucket containing two others. Cade noted their bigger size—caught by his dad, not his own handiwork—and closed the lid. "That heron take our food?" he asked.

Haven shook his head, as his face found a smile.

"What's so funny? I caught the fish," Cade said, unsure of what he'd missed.

Haven pointed at the open-faced jar of trout eggs—their fishing bait.

"Ohh . . ." Cade's voice trailed off.

"No worries. That was trout bait. Not *our* food, young man. We won't go hungry this morning, no siree."

"But, how'll we fish for more browns?" Cade asked, his voice squeaking on the last word.

"Those fish are so hungry they'd probably bite an empty hook to see if it was something good. Besides, you're the angler, the outdoorsman. No fish is safe in these waters," Haven added.

"You're just saying that to make me feel better. I messed up. The day's blown, ain't it?"

Cade looked from the fast-moving current to the high-falling water above Spoonbill Dam—spurting from the open slots on the side of all that concrete.

"As long as there's water falling, there'll be fish," Haven said. "The *Explorer Extraordinaire* never quits looking for *Adventure*."

Cade admired and hated how his dad could say something and not really say anything at the same time. It was something he was blessed with. He wasn't afraid of anything, especially herons eating their bait.

As if reading Cade's mind, Haven added, "Besides, if I catch that heron he'll make one great piece of taxidermy, won't he?"

The two sat on the shore and let the mist from the cascading water, slipping over the high edge of the dam, tickle their faces. The molecules of hydrogen and oxygen spilled onto them, wetting the ground around their bodies ever so gradually. Cade kept wiping his face as his dad watched the water.

"I wish this was every Saturday, don't you?"

Cade was unsure of what part of *this* he meant; he gave a non-committal shrug.

"Why do you think I come down here with you, anyways?" Haven pried.

"To get away from Mom?"

"Naw. I love Mom. You know that. And you."

"To work?"

Haven shook his head, but the smile remained plastered on, as if God carved him from stone with that look.

"It *is* work, ain't it? You want to be around the dam 24/7."

"I'd never love work as much as I do you and your mom. You *know* that. Or . . . at least I hope you do."

Cade exhaled, a frown on his face.

"But, I won't lie. I do love coming down here. Seeing you wrestle trout. Watching the herons make away with our bait. And this." Haven spanned his hand out to the two-hundred-and-fifty-something-foot-tall dam above them. "I love this monster. Every bit of it."

"You're weird," Cade said, but he was drawn to the structure as well. The smooth limestone rocks, and the water lapping at the edges of the dam were serene.

"But, I love what's under it even more," Haven added, eyes focused on the murky green pool of ripples and bubbles – his past as a Kentucky coalminer always a factor in his adventures, Cade knew.

Pretend images of caves and abandoned school buses and catfish the size of his basketball goal at home made Cade shiver. He recalled the horror stories of classmates at Seton. Quinsey Bates, his best friend, always teased him that these catfish could pull a man, woman, or Sasquatch under and hold them until they drowned.

*Drowning.*

Cade's single biggest fear, because he didn't know how to swim. (Or, more so had been scared out of the water after nearly drowning once.) The notion of wading and fly-fishing in such currents scared him to death, but with his dad there, it made it slightly more bearable.

"The caves," he heard himself say. The image of a cave his dad found alongside a bluff at the lake brought back fond memories of the two finding geodes and shouting at all the crazy bats.

"Sure. There're caves down there," Haven said, pointing to the bottom of the dam's structure. "And all sorts of other things you'd want to explore. But first, we have to teach you to swim *better*."

Haven reached over to Cade like he might toss him into deep water. Cade tensed up suddenly.

"We just need to spend a weekend splashing around like we used to."

Cade let the swimming talk drop and drifted off to thoughts of what rested below Spoonbill Dam; bluegill moving around dead bodies and forgotten burial mounds.

Haven stood up and popped his back. He groaned and leaned over and offered a hand. "I'm gonna go check on those leaks, son. I told Mr. Almon I'd look at 'em before we left."

Cade started to say *Don't go because . . .* but realized it was a silly request.

"Now, we'll learn how to swim and be Adventurers, and before you know it, I'll show you how to dive and underwater weld like I do. Deal?"

"I get to weld?"

"Of course. As long as you don't pull any hotshot maneuvers a hundred feet down," Haven kidded.

The depth of one hundred feet felt all too real.

"The seepage in the limestone is bothering Almon and the Corps of Engineers. I better go help. It'll help us save up for a vacation. We can finally go to the ocean. Won't your mom like that?"

Cade felt his dad gently pinch and shake his triceps. Then, he walked around the base of the dam and started the slow ascent up to the dam's main platform. Here, Cade imagined, Haven would gather his underwater welding equipment and plunge into the crisp, cool depths of Cumberland Lake.

# CHAPTER TWO

Cade dozed off, and the next thing he knew he awoke to what sounded like a war zone above the Spoonbill floodgates on the main level. There were sirens and lights flashing from their fixtures on the sides of the dam. A sonorous horn blared over and over again. Cade heard a recorded voice saying, "Please stand back," repeatedly. He scanned the tops of the dam for some sign, some explanation.

There was a tall, broad-shouldered man descending the bank toward Cade. The man looked directly at him, his stride firm and purposeful. He came over to where Cade stood on shaky knees, reached out and placed his hand on the teen's shoulder.

"We have to get you out of here, son," the man said. "Haven would want you to go with me," he added.

"You know Dad?" Cade said, finding his voice. "Why isn't he back?"

The man quickly introduced himself as Mr. Almon, Haven's boss. He kept his hand at rest on Cade's shoulder and exhaled. "Life makes a fool out of most of us. I never thought it would do it to him . . ."

*What was he talking about?*

"Calm down, boy," Almon said, as Cade began to buck under that terrible, heavy hand. "And ease up on my shirt, will ya?"

Cade looked at the long-sleeved shirt he was bunching up and threatening to rip off the old man. His hand was coiled around the material tight.

"Let's get you to the top. They're sending divers right now. He should've resurfaced already," Almon added.

Cade ghost-walked ahead of the aging supervisor up Spoonbill Dam and onto the platform area. He peered over the edge of the dam and into the rich, deep blue-green waters of the mighty Cumberland—a lake formerly known and named for its large spoonbill (or, paddlefish populations). His fear of water was intensified by the news he'd heard, and what it could mean. Mr. Almon's words had been like the deep, murky water – hard to divine and foreboding.

Cade couldn't (and wouldn't) accept anything until he had proof.

"Don't lean too far, or you'll end up on the news. Haven told me you couldn't swim too well. I still don't see how you get out into that current like you do, if you can hardly swim and all." His voice fell away.

"Huh?"

The two sank into silence as divers arrived on the dam's platform, eagerly requesting information from Almon. He started to give them a long, detailed history of the dam's first leaks, seeps, and accounts of limestone withering. The lead diver, medium build, with thinning, brown hair held up his hand, barking out the words, "Quickly, old man!"

"He was at the base repairing a steel fixture around 10:00 a.m. and—"

"Wet welding?" the diver asked.

"No. Dry underwater welding. What do you think? He was at the base! Of course he was wet welding that far down!" Mr. Almon's face flushed.

Cade now saw the concern on Almon's face; something he'd missed earlier. He fought back tears as he watched Almon argue with the stranger.

"What happened?" another diver chimed in, flipper smacking the concrete pavement. "We need to get in there, Bill," he said to the man calling the shots.

"I know that. Listen, if you're not telling us something that might be dangerous to *our* health, then I'm holding you personally responsible," the first diver added, pointing a gloved, diving finger into Almon's chest.

"All I know is Haven never messes up. He goes down with plenty of oxygen every time. Plenty of supplies. *Loves welding.* This is his boy . . . right here," bringing Cade over for inspection.

The lead diver must've noticed Cade's expression, because the questions stopped. He shouted, "Dive gear on!" to his team, and turned from the pair to face the water. The divers waddled to the edge of the platform, and on the lead diver's command, all five plunged into the placid water.

***

Risks.

There were risks with everything the Rainy family did. It's why Hollie always displayed a shocked, finger-in-the-electrical-socket look. The Rainy males were unpredictable. Cade, at thirteen, had learned plenty of his dad's tricks. Life is meant to be lived, not watched! Haven would proclaim on any (and all) vacations. He drove anything with a motor at full speed, the lawnmower included. He once drove them through the entire state of Georgia in less than four hours.

This is why the waiting was so difficult for Cade. Bubbles came to the surface as the divers navigated the endless depths of water. Cade reached out to pluck a bubble and imagined his dad saying, "Careful, son."

Instinctively, he reached his hand back into the safety of the dam's platform. He spun around and expected to see Mr. Almon, but he was gone. Cade squinted up at the concrete rooms where the U.S. Army Corps of Engineers facilitated the movements of the water levels day and night. He saw a shadow and realized it was Almon barking into a telephone. Cade thought he overheard the words "You'll pay!" but wasn't sure, since the water and turbines made so much noise around the dam's base.

Mr. Almon reappeared at the door, and he approached Cade, offering his hand like a kind grandpa. Cade recoiled. "What's the word?" He wanted to sound strong, bold like his dad.

"God willing, we'll know something when those divers resurface," Almon said, pointing to the bubbles.

Ten. Fifteen minutes went by. Then, twenty minutes passed, and not one diver reappeared. Cade started to watch the hazy orange sunshine in the summer sky. He would do anything to take his mind from the absence of Haven. Blue herons congregated at the edge of the divers' bubbles, expecting dinner, Cade imagined. The sight of so many herons made him recall their earlier predicament, when a fishing trip being cut short was their only worry.

The pesky birds restored a little of his hope. If they could wait so patiently, then so could he. Mr. Almon found a comfortable concrete slab and sat down. "Take a seat," he encouraged.

"I'm fine. Dad'll be fine, too," Cade said. "You'll see. How long has he worked for you?"

"As long as he's been a welder ... fifteen years, I guess. Give or take. Because he started before you were born." Almon said it as if he knew every detail of Cade's life, like he had counted the very hairs on his head.

Cade shook away from the man and peered out at a neighboring fishery—an adjacent platform.

"Those trout are big enough to mount on your wall, when we let them drop down the floodgates." Almon laughed, trying to change the subject.

"We caught three earlier. Not near that big," Cade said. "Dad's were bigger than mine."

"If you left them in that bucket down there, they're dead. Trout need a lot of oxygen," he said without pause.

The word *dead* hung in the air like a cold front that didn't intend to move. Cade tried to wave it away. "Fishing here on Saturdays is our thing," Cade said.

"I see you two all the time . . . from up here." Almon indicated the platform. "He's a good man."

"I know."

***

The calm water's surface was suddenly shattered. The divers reappeared one at a time like turtles coming up for sunlight, a log to rest on. Cade watched them climb onto the platform. One through five, all of the divers returned—present, accounted for—except for Haven.

*Good one!* Cade thought but didn't say aloud. Another prank from the *Explorer Extraordinaire,* his dad. But as the masks and air tubes came off each man—and the last one heaved for air—there was an eerie silence.

When their breathing steadied, Cade said, "Well, I'd like to know where he is." His voice shaking and squeaky—the fear suddenly palpable.

No one spoke.

Then, the lead diver finally stepped up to Cade. "It's dark down there, boy. Pitch black. I mean it. Can't see nothin'."

Cade gave him his best dumb look; the diver looked away. There was silence, and even the herons dispersed when the bubbles went away. The turbines were the only noise now, and they were monotonous and rhythmic to the point of being unnoticed. Cade, lost in thought and worry, just stared blankly ahead.

"Well, if he's not with you, he must be down there still. Probably wanting to give us all a good scare. He might've found a new cave. We found one once—"

"Haven wouldn't do that. Not like this," Almon said, and Cade knew it was true. Even his father wouldn't cause his friends and family to worry.

The other four divers looked to the ground, awaiting direction from their leader. He nodded for them to go inside. As they traipsed away, he looked Cade directly in the eyes, and said, without hesitation, "We know where the equipment is. We found the parts: light, helmet, welding rod, power cords, cables and hoses. We just didn't find *him* yet," he added sheepishly.

The word *yet* stymied some of Cade's doubts. He focused on the equipment the diver mentioned. "Bring it up," he said.

"We will in a bit."

"No. Now!" Cade's emboldened teen voice squawked.

"Okay. I'll go down and get it." He tried to muss Cade's hair, but the boy backed away.

The diver turned to Almon. "It was probably electric shock. Insulation was wrong, or . . . the current was off, and he didn't tell the surface operator in time—"

"Not in front of the boy!" Almon hissed. "And no, it's none of those things. Haven didn't make those kinds of mistakes," the old man confirmed, adding, "I've always been his surface operator. Always. He didn't alert me at all. So you're wrong. Now do as the boy said and get that gear!"

The diver was caught off-guard, and he backed away awkwardly. He fell into the water and put his mask on sideways. The man dove straight to the bottom and retrieved the items.

Again, he returned for a second time without any trace of Haven Rainy.

# CHAPTER THREE

Headlight, helmet, and welding rod were all at Cade's feet.

He carried them inside the rustic, brick lakefront home and waited for his mom, Hollie, to say something. Anything. The tall, arched entryway dwarfed them where they stood.

When she opened her petite, thin-lipped mouth, it wasn't to encourage him. Her lips trembled. Hollie's brown hair fell into her face, and she tried to wipe it away, but the tears made it impossible. Cade was as tall as her.

He remembered Haven more than once holding his fingers to her red mouth and shushing her worries away. Cade knew he couldn't do the same.

"Mom?" Cade said, finding his voice. "I'm going to keep them."

The headlight and helmet were still damp to the touch. Beneath his fingernails, he saw the dried slime and dirt from the trout he'd caught that morning.

"The welding rod stays outside in the shed," she added, pointing to the well-worn, white paint-chipped building in their backyard.

Cade knew not to cross her; he was too tired to resist anyways. He set the items down and carried the welding tool outside and into the old storage room. When he returned, his mother was sitting motionless on the couch like a zombie, staring blankly into the cushions where Haven sat earlier.

Cade had heard her scolding him about the fish smell. His dad had planted a big kiss on her.

"Mmm," Haven had declared loud enough for everyone to hear that morning. "If those breakfast sandwiches taste this good, the trip will be almost as good as being right here with you . . . almost."

"You better bring yourself back here in one piece. And keep that smell outside," she'd added, holding her nose.

Now, she stared at the empty cushion, which still held his indentation in the green, plush fabric.

"The *Explorer Extraordinaire* never quits looking for *Adventure*," Cade recited from his dad's long-time expression, his voice emotionless now.

"He's not coming back," Hollie's voice echoed lonely throughout the room. "… ever, Cade. Do you hear me?"

Her unfamiliar tone gave him a shiver, and he shook and couldn't get himself to stop. The doorbell rang and both jumped.

There were two knocks on the metal, storm door.

Neither got up.

"Mrs. Rainy? Cade? Please open up," a tired, tender voice said.

There was a bright flash, and thunder cracked across the sky outside. The inside of the house was suddenly illuminated, and the *boom* was loud enough to jar the chandelier above them.

"Please? I'm getting drenched out here," the voice rose above the roar.

Cade didn't recall a cloud in the sky earlier. But then, he didn't recall much after the diver only brought up his dad's equipment. Now, the sky was littered with lightning bolts. Water spilling from above and emptying into the sewers outside. Then, it was carried down and down and eventually would find its way into the lake.

Hollie opened the door slowly for a rain-soaked, hooded Mr. Almon. With him was the lead diver from earlier, who looked completely different without the black wetsuit, oxygen tank, and goggles. He extended his hand to Cade, "Bill Mulvaney. I meant to introduce myself earlier, but you understand."

"Bill, this is Mrs. Hollie Rainy," Mr. Almon said.

Hollie's hand shook noticeably as she extended it. The *Mrs.* felt lonely being broadcast as it was to the mournful room. "Obliged for your help," she said.

Mr. Almon cleared his throat. "Uh, listen Hollie. Bill and his group were wanting to keep the cords, cables, and hoses for a bit more inspection. They want to see if . . . ahh there was a rupture in any of them. Anything at all. And, they want to be thorough so that—"

She waved her hand at Almon, and then she covered her eyes and lowered her head. Cade saw tears hit the faux hardwood floor, and he went to grab his mom's hand.

Hollie wrapped Cade in a big hug, bigger than he imagined possible for her slender, five-foot frame. She let her tear-streaked eyes drip onto his curly, blond head.

"They just want to help, Mom," Cade encouraged. "Bill will look into it. Another *Adventure*. It's what Dad—"

"Hush that talk!" she snapped. "There won't be talk of adventures again, for a long while. Adventures are what got us here. Don't you see?"

None of the men spoke. Bill stared at the chandelier, which was made of plastic, not crystal.

Mr. Almon cleared his throat again and reached into his pocket for an envelope he'd tried to keep dry, despite the storm's relentless efforts. Cade saw it was only semi-saturated as Almon tried to give it to her.

She held onto Cade and buried him against her chest. The tears didn't seem to let up, much like the rain.

No one moved for the outstretched letter.

Finally, Almon said, "I'll just place this over here." His voice sounded a little choked up; or, it might've been his constant need to clear his throat. Cade couldn't tell.

"Thank you, Cade, for being so strong," Almon offered, and grabbed Bill by his elbow, turning the two and opening the door, all in one smooth motion. As he did, wind blew into the home, knocking pieces of the plastic, clear chandelier along with a single family picture frame clanking onto the wooden foyer floor.

# CHAPTER FOUR

There were opened boxes everywhere. Items half-in and half-out of each one; none were labeled. Cade accidentally sent one toppling to the floor from his bedside table. When he stooped to pick it up, his mom entered.

"He rises," she said, her voice thick and hoarse.

"And falls," Cade tried to joke, as he fell back into the sheets. He wanted to keep her spirits high. It didn't feel real that his dad was gone. He expected to get a summons for Sunday church at any moment. Dad never missed a service, and by default, none of them did either. He knew his dad had been the catalyst for seeking love and mercy. It wasn't that Hollie was against a Creator, but she just didn't pick up faith like Haven did.

"Was there a box sale?" Cade tried to tease.

"We're moving today," Hollie spoke flatly.

Cade pursed his lips to let another question spill out, but it didn't. He knew she was hiding her true emotions. She was *trying* to keep their world turning. Her red eyes showed defeat. He reached to hug her, but she moved away. His mom raised the mini-blinds and let the sun, now restored from the night's storm, cast its other-worldly heat onto them. Cade felt sweat cling to his skin, his clothes, and the covers. He pushed them off, onto the floor.

"All these boxes. Where are we—"

"Across town. Away from *this*," she muttered, eyes downcast, finger pointing in the direction of the mighty Cumberland. "It's brought us enough pain. I don't want to see it . . . or smell it, ever again."

The reminder of Dad was too much. It hadn't always been that way, Cade thought. She used to love going fishing at the lake; she was great at waterskiing behind the Bayliner. Hollie could even drop one and slalom ski, if she wanted. But, she didn't want to now, Cade saw. She wanted to be far, far away.

So, they scooped up box after box of kitchen appliances, home décor, lawn equipment, and his dad's underwater welding tools. When he tried to place them into the old, rusting Dodge Caravan, Hollie said, "Not those. We don't need it. Just like we don't need *that*," she said, pointing to the dusty Bayliner still covered in the shed.

"Dad's gear. Of course, I'm taking it," Cade said, holding it close to his chest. It was unfathomable to leave it behind—a sin if there ever was one in his or her life. To his surprise, she didn't argue.

"Well, get that *stuff* and put it in that old cardboard box. I don't want to run across it again. You hear?" her voice shook. "And you can put it away someplace safe when we get where we're going. Out of sight. And that thing . . . it stays," she said, as she closed the shed door, leaving the abandoned boat for the next person.

***

Cade did a lot of soul-searching as the boxes were toted across Seton, Kentucky—to a fifty-acre ranch Hollie's family still owned, her grandmother's. It had sat empty since she passed nine years prior. Now, there were white sheets over all the furniture, a window still broken. There were leaves scattered all around the room. *The* cardboard box was opened last, and Cade made sure his mom didn't see him open it, or place the helmet, headlight, and welding rod in a different storage unit beside the ranch home. He patted the welding utensil. "God, help us find Dad. If not, I trust you're taking good care of him. Amen."

Cade inspected the expansive first floor—almost three thousand square feet. Cade walked from room to room and checked out the space and listened to how the empty rooms echoed. Meanwhile, Hollie set boxes down and filled up what would soon become their new lives. When he tired, Cade helped unpack and watched his mom choose where things went. After a few deliberations on her part, he saw it didn't matter where things went. They'd never be the same without Dad.

"Breakfast for dinner, since we missed it earlier?" she asked, her voice mousy and barely above a whisper.

Cade tried to nod his head, let her know that he could fake caring about meals, as she needed him to. But, he didn't want to eat. Nothing ever seemed like it would taste good again. She saw his eyes filling with tears. "Cade. Cade. Don't let those blues get all red. We can't change a thing about what happened. What's done is done."

Cade grabbed her hand. "God'll help us," he tried to encourage. He wanted to be the man, or, as much of one as he could.

"We'll see," his mom echoed. "I surely hope so . . ."

The new home didn't have a clock, and Cade couldn't find one in any of the boxes. Had time stopped? It felt as if it had. Maybe the world was never going to begin again, he thought. If it didn't he'd be okay with that, except for the endless amount of blank space he'd have on his hands. His thoughts were what bothered him. Maybe he could've saved his dad, if he'd been awake. But, he knew better.

First, he couldn't swim that well.

Second, his dad was in much better hands going into the water with Mr. Almon, than anyone else.

And if anyone could find him, it was Bill Mulvaney and his divers. Those five had helped recover hundreds of souls from Cumberland.

Cade heard a beeping inside one of the boxes; he dug in and retrieved a wristwatch he never wore. It read 8:11 p.m., but it hadn't been adjusted in years. It could've been right on the dot or off by an hour or more, depending on daylight savings, malfunctions, etc. It was one thing to lose his dad, but to not even know what time it was somehow made him feel like a ghost.

"Mom! What time is it?!" he shouted across the large home. "MOM!"

"What?! I'm right here," she said, standing just behind Cade. "Where's your cellphone?" she answered. "It'll have the time."

He could've smacked himself for being so slow-witted; he pulled the cell from his pocket, the Galaxy S his dad recommended when they went to get their phones just a month ago. He'd said, "An *Adventure* needs direction. The *Explorer* needs something capable of leading him out of any tight space. Sometimes technology can help!" Then, he'd handed Cade a phone and got himself one, too. Haven had insisted on water-proofing everything. He'd said, once outside the cell store, "Now, we'll never get lost. Even if we're climbing down into a nasty cave filled with black water."

Cade took the phone and checked the battery. Half of the juice was gone. He turned it over in his hand. Thirteen years old and he felt like an orphan now.

His dad was the last call in his phone log. The emptiness of the foyer and living room—without his dad's voice, his strong laughter—made him instinctively push 'call' on the phone screen.

Cade listened to the empty, steady rings, his dad's voice saying: *If I missed you, it's because I'm loving life too much to stop. I'll call you back,* and then the beep came to leave a message. Cade held the phone cradled against his ear and waited for the voice message to time itself out.

As much as he tried, he couldn't force himself to speak into the void.

# CHAPTER FIVE

Hollie cleaned the house religiously. The constant cleaning made Cade nervous. *Maybe she needs some alone time?* He figured it was none of his business—having just settled himself, somewhat—and felt the need to go outside, explore.

Just the word *explore* tore him up. He doubted whether he'd ever see the world as being marvelous ever again. The blue skies were tinted with ochre as the sun rose. His dad called the mornings and evenings *God's crayon box*. It was a time when everything was being colored in and set apart again. He'd told Cade that nights were when everything ran together and dreams overtook them. Cade didn't have a problem with nights. He slept through those.

A truck pulled up, the sound of gravel crunching caused Cade to stop daydreaming. It was a step-side Ford pick-up. His dad had always said, "Buying a Ford is like asking for a hailstorm." Cade remembered Chevy bow ties plastering everything his dad owned. The unfamiliar truck made him wary.

"How do, young man?" the flannel-wearing, aged driver said, craning his neck out to look at the gravel beneath him. His skin was a muddy brown color, and he had deep creases from too much sun. "It came a frog-drowner yesterday, didn't it?"

Cade stared at the gravel. Afraid to look up at the wispy, gray-headed man, who couldn't be younger than seventy.

"The driveway. You've let her all but wash away to kingdom come." He spat some tobacco juice down onto the rivulets the driveway held from the water gullies. "I'd say you'd find limestone pebbles all the way across the county from this one lot," the man said.

"That's where we're from," Cade blurted, unsure of himself. "Across the county . . . next to Cumberland Lake."

The old man hung an elbow outside the truck and extended his left hand for an awkward handshake. "I'm Abbott Mize. You can call me Abbott or Mize. Please don't say Mr. Mize. That just sounds weird."

"Ca-Cade," the boy stuttered. "Mom's inside."

"Y'all just pulled in last night," he said. "Saw all the commotion from over there." He pointed. "That's me. Way off in the distance. See that house?"

Cade couldn't see anything really. God had strewn what looked to be every crayon in the box across the morning sky. He cupped his hand over his eyes, as his dad had taught him, and peered at the small, blurry dot dozens of acres away.

"I'm your nearest, dearest neighbor." The old man laughed and coughed.

Cade looked to the front door for Mom; she didn't appear to be anywhere inside.

"Listen. I know about what happened," Abbott said, boring holes into Cade's unwashed Batman T-shirt. "In a town this small, there's no hiding. And that's okay. I just wanted to introduce myself. Tell you about your driveway. If you need help, I'd be most obliged."

"We can do it ourselves," Cade said. "I just need a . . . a . . . rake or something."

Abbott didn't react if he thought the idea ludicrous or not. Cade added, "Maybe a strong water hose to wash it all back into place. I—"

"That's something. I can see those rocks resettling just like they used to be," Abbott said, not scolding Cade at all.

Cade knew it was dumb the moment the words left him. Washing rocks back into their original places? Really? "Never mind," he said, turning to go back inside his hollow, creaky-floored home.

"Hey, Cade," he said, the name sounding more like *Cayuhd* as he said it. "I want to help. Honest I do. We can get started on this driveway in no time. I can go get my animals fed and be back by noon."

"We don't need help. Thanks anyway, *Mr. Mize,*" Cade said, intentionally defying the neighbor's request, walking back inside with loud stomps.

***

Abbott Mize was outside clanging around the driveway on the oddest thing Cade had ever seen. He was riding a lawnmower going up and down the driveway. The mower had a used mattress spring—without padding, just coils—clanging up and down behind it. There were large stones stacked across the mattress coils to keep it from jumping too high. Abbott bumped up and down the driveway swinging the coils around and around.

Cade, brazened by Mize's return, marched across the lawn to the driveway and yanked the wheel of the mower—to try and hold Mize in place. The old man braked and took his bubble-shaped ear protectors off. He turned the mower down, then off, shouting, "Looks good, huh?"

Cade was too mad to look at the driveway. This new home was his responsibility, he figured. "Get out of here!"

"Son, I'm just trying to help y'all out. There's not enough rakes in Seton to carry out here and clean up this mess. Lemme finish this lap, and you can have all the fun you want washing it back into place." His eyes roved the driveway.

The front door creaked open and shut. Before either knew she was there, Hollie had Cade by the ear. "Whaddya think you're doing?! This man—"

"Abbott Mize, ma'am," the old man said.

"Mr. Mize was just trying—"

"He doesn't like to be called Mr. Mize," Cade spat.

"Abbott was just trying to do a neighborly good deed. Isn't that right?" Hollie said, releasing Cade's ear. "We need all of the kindness we can get. Now that your dad—"

"Listen Mrs. Rainy. I heard what happened, and I felt I should come introduce myself. I live way over yonder," said Abbot, again pointing at the small, black speck of a home. "Y'all are welcome over for dinner anytime you like. Anytime."

Abbott reached for the key switch to crank the mower back to life but hesitated. "I was thinking . . ."

"Yes?" Hollie said.

"I have a lot, and I mean, a lot of chores. Almost too many for a man at fifty-five."

Cade didn't believe him. He had to be every bit of seventy. The wrinkles, calloused hands, and hair were that of a much older man.

"I was wondering if this boy of yours . . . er, young man, might be able to help me with a fence I'm piddling on and trying to build before winter."

"Cade doesn't know much about fence-building, but I'm sure he could try. He's a hard worker and a good boy. He helped his dad--"

"I don't want to help, Mom. He already helped himself to our driveway. Why would I go over there and help him?"

"Because you can learn a thing or two about living around here. We'll need it, if we get another storm like yesterday."

"It came a belly-washer, didn't it?" Abbott encouraged. "I couldn't see a thing on my porch. It filled my boots plumb up with rain water, and they weren't even on the edge of the porch." He laughed and smacked the lawnmower's hood, then recoiled from the heat of the motor.

"What do you farm?" Hollie asked.

"Lil of this and that. Some tobacco when it gets enough rain. Like last night."

"I saw some horses over there, too, I thought," she said. "Quarter horses?"

"You have good eyes, ma'am," Abbott said, tipping his imaginary hat at her. "Quarter horses my wife and kids used to ride, before they left. Moved to Nashville. The bright lights and all," his eyes looking distant, as he said it.

"She just left?" Cade blurted out, forgetting his anger.

"She could sing like a dream. Even had the name for country music. Cordelia Darby. People said she sounded like Tammy Wynette and Tanya Tucker blended into one. I guess she took them at their word. 'Cuz she left months ago and took Dalton and Tisha with her. Guess I'll wait till she writes me at Christmas time, because some of us can't just up and leave Kentucky to make it big, can we?"

Cade had been too quick to judge the man. Fifty-five and looking seventy from all the farm work and his family leaving, too. He knew pain, Cade saw. "I'll help with your fence," he said.

Abbott shook the boy's hand with his right paw this time from his mower seat. "Welcome to the neighborhood," the last word sounding more like *neighbyhood*.

With that Abbott placed his ear protectors back onto his head, made one more lap with the odd contraption, and left, leaving neat little vacuum-like marks along the driveway. Cade admitted it looked a lot better with the rocks distributed more evenly than they were earlier. He didn't tell his mom this, but her face showed the same satisfaction.

"Let's eat something," she said. "A working man has to rest some, too, if he's going to put up a fence tomorrow."

Cade walked in step with his mom into the house, and without Dad, it seemed like life on another planet. One where strange men told stories and used phrases he'd never heard. It was a flatter space away from all that water, away from the churning Cumberland.

# CHAPTER SIX

The next morning Cade was up before the rooster crowed. Before God colored the sky. It was one week until his last year of middle school.

"Grab that post hole digger there," Abbott ordered, his voice not unkind, even at six in the morning. It was just gruff, raspy like it was when he cleared his throat. "We'll be on our way."

"How many acres do you have, Mize? We have about fifty, Mom says."

"Not near that. See, your land runs all the way up to this line," he said, pointing to a fence beside them. "You have all of it. My piece of land is only about twelve acres, but plenty when your family leaves you high and dry, huh?" His attempt at humor falling flat. "I just need us to repair this fence so that the horses won't get out. Especially that one there: Clay. He's a handful. Why, that ol' gelding would hop a fence just for sport. I love him, but he's as feisty as if he'd never been castrated."

"Castrated?"

"Aw, never mind. It's not important. We just need to get the barrier back up, before he's in your pasture pestering you. Sound good?"

Cade felt his head bob up and down, but he was too busy thinking about how much more land they had than this man who actually *used* his for farming. Fifty versus twelve. It was just land in Mom's family. They'd never even had to work for it. The thought made him feel a little guilty.

"You listening?"

"Yes sir," Cade responded automatically.

"I don't need that. I'm not much older than your mom. Besides, I want us to be more like business partners. You do your share of work and I'll do mine. We're equal. Whaddya say?"

"Deal," Cade said. He looked around at the twelve acres and knew it would be a long day. Holding the wooden handles and trying to wiggle them in and out to get a feel for the motion he'd be doing vexed him. "Like this?" he asked, thwacking the metal mouth of the digger into the ground, pulling the handles as far apart as the earth's semi-dry resistance would allow.

"We have a regular farmhand in our midst, don't we?" Abbott said in the direction of Clay, the gelding. The horse shook his mane back and forth like he understood. "Just one thing," Abbott added. "When you plunge those steel limbs into the ground, be sure to go straight down north to south and then rock the ground back and forth like this to make sure you're picking up as much as you can when you clamp the metal together. Okay? Otherwise, you're just like Clay there—spinning your wheels. Here, let me show you." And he did. Abbott lifted the wooden handles an arm's length above his head, drove the metal tongs down into the rain-softened ground, wiggled the tool back and forth, then pried the hands as far apart as he could, and lifted the large mound of dirt from the ground.

"My hands hurt already," Cade whined, after only a few tries. "Isn't there something else we can use?"

"I knew I should've hired a body builder," Abbott spat, brown juice landing in the vicinity of Clay's hoof. The gelding leaned down and sniffed at the odd smell, twitched his nose in the air, repulsed by its sweet aroma.

"I'll be fine. Just maybe do you have gloves or something? Blisters have started up already."

"Yes, heavens yes," he said, smacking his forehead. "I meant to get those. That was the one thing I didn't aim to leave at the house. Here, I'll be right back," he added, turning to the well-worn farmhouse door.

Shapes that had been distorted in the dark shadows of early morning were coming into plainer sight. It was always astounding to Cade how quickly the sun rose over southern Kentucky. The sun seemed to jump out of its hiding place all within thirty minutes of morning.

Abbott walked back outside and stretched and yawned loudly. The sound carried for miles, it seemed. When he was beside Cade, he handed a worn pair of cowhide gloves to his new neighbor. "We won't work with barbed wire yet. So, I don't expect these will be ruin't, huh?"

His tone made Cade realize how much he treasured, no, took care of things. Maybe he didn't have a lot of things, if the house was any indication.

"I'll keep them as clean as possible," Cade joked. "Now, I do it like *this*?" He dug straight down and leveraged out a perfect hole in three swift efforts.

"Well, I swear. I couldn't have taught myself any faster," Abbott joked. "You keep that up, and we'll be out of the sun before it heats up. I'm gonna go check on that silly horse. Make sure he hasn't found any new strands of barbed wire to hurt himself with. Holler if you need me." Abbott walked a few yards away.

Cade heard the horse nicker and saw Abbott brushing the hair out of the gelding's eyes a moment later. The two were obviously used to one another. Like an old couple, they spoke with brevity as Clay answered Abbott's words with snorts and tosses of his head. It was funny to Cade. Farm living. If this is what it was, it didn't seem so bad.

He created perfect holes on the first three spots where a wooden post would soon go. The gloves helped with his grip and protected the quickly forming blisters beneath. By the fourth and fifth post, the three-count was becoming more like six. Cade knocked against limestone on the eighth hole with a jarring *claaaang!* His arms shook, and he almost knocked himself in the eye with the rounded, wooden handle, when it recoiled against the rock.

"Hey, champ! It doesn't have to be built today," Abbott said. "I know it'll get hot, but we have time. I gave Clay some sugar cubes.

He should calm himself down a bit. Here, let me have a go at it. I'm still fresh," Abbott coaxed.

"How many holes are there to dig?" Cade asked, pausing at the eighth. "Does it go all the way around here? All twelve acres?"

"Have you ever seen one that didn't end where it started?" Abbott asked.

"Nope."

Abbott laughed. "Neither have I. It wraps around these two fields. Tobacco and horses. One post every ten feet, for a little over six hundred feet. Then, that row up the middle there to divide the two. But we can stop whenever you want to. This isn't a race or anything. Even though it feels like it with the humidity."

The blisters popped, rubbing against the cowhide. Cade finished the eighth hole and finally handed the post diggers to Abbott.

"May I have those, too?" Abbott asked, requesting the gloves.

"How'd you get so good at farming?"

"Lots and lots of practice, buddy," Abbott dug down with the digger as he spoke. "I've gotten to where I can multi-task better than I ever thought . . . Cordelia leaving and all. I guess it's a blessing and a curse. You know?"

Cade didn't answer at first. He thought about the fancy tractors he'd seen farmers use in other parts of the county. They always looked to be going somewhere with loads of hay and straw. He knew there were better means than this one. "Why not use a tractor? I've seen ones that burrow out a hole in no time," Cade said, proud of himself.

"Yeah. They can. I've seen 'em too. They cost a pretty penny. Too much if you ask me. How much do you think a gadget like that costs?"

"Probably a lot," Cade answered.

"Bingo. I don't know folks who have 'em who would be willing to let me borrow 'em anyways," he said. "Seton's few wealthy folks don't part with their *good* stuff. Even for a minute."

"Sorry I brought it up," Cade said.

"Besides, I don't need any of that. We have you," Abbott said, looking behind at the previous holes. "Here, take your time, and I'm going to go get the posts and put 'em in place for the first ones. When you get tired, rest. I'll dig as many as I can during the mid-day heat. We'll drink spring water when we need it. I've got a spring I draw from, and it tastes better than anything you've ever had."

With that, Abbott found and placed the posts beside their handiwork. Cade dug the ground until his hands felt like they were bleeding. He looked down and saw they *were* bleeding. Abbott still had the gloves. Cade was now on hole twelve and didn't think he could handle the impact of one more heave. He set the diggers down and walked away from the fence.

Abbott wiped at his forehead, his shaggy gray-white hair. "There." He exhaled. "The posts are in place for the time being. Feel free to help yourself to that water. It's in a basin on the back porch. There's a big dipper there, and it's cold, because I just brought it up from the spring this morn'."

Cade half-saluted Abbott and turned for the house, sore hands shaking. He looked back and saw Abbott not missing a beat. He picked up the diggers and was already moving down to number twelve to finish Cade's attempt. The sun had risen to its peak, as Cade staggered inside the house.

***

There were little effects on the walls of the wood-paneled home. It was quaint in its design and adornments. Cade found that Cordelia and the kids' departure must've taken most of the life—the memories—with it. There were a few pictures of the family, one with Abbott hoisting his daughter into the air—big grins on both faces. He walked down the hallway, which opened into the kitchen, where he saw a table with dust on its top. It looked undisturbed since they'd left over six months ago. Cade turned and found the door to the back porch. Here, he saw the metal tin pan with gallons of water in it. There was a big ladle hanging on a nail. Cade took it and scooped into the water and brought it to his lips. He drank so quickly the water spilled over and onto the floor. The water was so cold. He didn't know it could be so cold and delicious. He dipped again and again. Six dips in all. When he stopped, he realized he'd overdone it.

Cade's stomach swelled as he placed the dipper back onto the wall and marched to the front of the house to sit on the porch—away from the sun's light. He found a metal glider and let the seat's motion carry him back and forth. The sloshing in his stomach continued as he rocked. He heard faintly, "Take a load off, buddy. I'll be over there in a minute."

Cade looked out and wiped sweat from his stinging eyes. The sun made everything dusty. Already it was so dry, even though the storm had hit last night. How could one part of the county be so different to the part he knew? Abbott dug one, two, three times, dropped the dirt with each plunge to the sides of the hole and moved to the next. Cade tried to count from the starting point. How many had he made past twelve? He found the one he'd quit on and there were at least that many more beyond it. How in the world?

"We'll have it dug in a few days!" Abbott yelled. "Won't we?"

"I have to go back to school in a week," Cade said, remembering the summer's end. It broke his heart to have to face the world so quickly, so soon after what happened at Spoonbill Dam with his dad.

"Ahh, yes. The place little people become big people. It does start back in Seton soon. I totally forgot. I guess not having *mine* around I—"

"We don't have to talk about it," Cade interrupted.

"I guess we don't. You'll be a high schooler, won't you? You're a big lad for your age," he said.

"Nope. I have one more year of middle. Luckily for me, Seton is all in the same building. So, I don't have to go anywhere else. Next year high school will be where middle school was," Cade added. "I'm happy I get another year of junior high though. Seems nice to be able to ease into—"

"I thought we weren't talking about it." Abbott's face spread into a smile; he knew he was funny, Cade imagined.

"We aren't," Cade said. "I guess we can just dig post holes until our hands fall off. Is that what you like best about living in the sticks?"

Abbott stroked the silver stubble breaking ground on his face and looked at the thirteen-year-old. "Maybe."

"I mean, I'm learning a lot. But, it seems like keeping a horse that doesn't want to be penned up, penned up all day, and digging posts for a fence that splits tobacco from the horses, is just something to keep your mind from wandering. It doesn't seem *fun*," Cade said. "Why do you do it, if it doesn't matter?"

"Fun. Hmm. That's a word I haven't said much since winter. I don't guess it's been much else except a distraction. You're right. Rebuilding this fence and watching Clay tear it down again and again has helped keep my mind from wandering to Cordelia and the kids. You're sharp for a middle schooler. You know that?" Abbott said, poking his thick fingers in Cade's side, making him squirm.

"Top of my class last year."

"Well, you have a lot of book smarts and some commonsense, too," Abbott encouraged. "Those two are a rare quality. Very few have it, and even fewer take it with 'em into adulthood."

Cade watched Clay paw and snort and stamp at the summer bugs—all but one horsefly flew away. He kept this up for a few minutes, and Abbott stood and said he was going to get a good long drink of water, too. When he returned, he told Cade about the farm, how it had been in his family three generations. Abbott mentioned how it was all he knew. City life and lake home living didn't interest him. Even if he never left Seton, Abbott said that raising tobacco and ornery geldings was plenty of company. He asked if Cade understood.

Cade flashed his eyes to the holes they'd dug and looked down at his throbbing hands. He said he was starting to understand something.

# CHAPTER SEVEN

The first day back and everything seemed suffocating and ridiculous.

Cade's best friend, Quinsey Bates, tanned and confident, told him who'd moved away from Seton, who was dating whom. He didn't mention Haven's death, and Cade wasn't bringing it up. No one else had broached the subject either. The school looked exactly the same as seventh grade. The seniors walked with swagger around the halls of the three-story schoolhouse. The juniors were brown-nosing them and the teachers they knew they'd have next year. The ninth & tenth graders tried to not get beat up. It was a constant battle for position.

Cade was pleased he had one more year in middle school. The second floor was calmer than the third. The sixth, seventh, & eighth graders ran around and giggled a lot. They still made absurd jokes and thought everything was meant to be taken lightly. Except his best friend, Quinn. He somehow had outgrown all of that, it seemed, over summer, because he said, "This is just baby stuff ain't it, man? Let's bail the first chance we get and grab a smoke."

*Grab a smoke?* "Smoke what?" Cade said, shocked by his friend's comment.

Quinsey laughed. "I like your style, Rainy. Smoke what?" He elbowed Cade. "Good one."

Cade winced. The pain from the post hole digging was still tight around his ribs. The farm labor had helped his physique though. Some of the girls were noticing. Quinn told him as much.

"We'll get the girls, champ! Don't you worry."

"What if I don't want them right now," Cade said, and admitted it was a lie—the second it left his mouth.

"Don't tell me you're going *that* way," Quinsey retorted. "We don't have *time* for that. Besides . . . I told you we're just friends, amigo." And he elbowed Cade again.

Cade waved him off, even though they walked to the same class. Seton's eighth grade class was only thirty-five students, and the school just opened up a dividing wall and permitted the entire class to take science, math, and so on, all in the same room. It created unity (and sometimes chaos). The first day back was never an exception. Students hustled about the room trying to be seen: Max with a new baseball card collection he was flashing about, Crawford with a lizard he'd caught at his house—claiming it was a salamander, Mercedes and Valerie showing off their tans, and the boys all watching. The teacher, one for all subjects this year, Ms. Easter, waited for an unprecedented quiet. But, the class fell short of her goal, as Crawford mentioned how the salamander swam in the lake behind his house. "Cumberland Lake," he said, "where Mr. Rainy drow—" and caught himself. The rest of Cade's classmates did likewise, all turning to stare at him.

"Welcome back," Ms. Easter said, with feigned interest in both their return and their summer experiences. She *did* glance at Cade quickly before she turned to her desk. "This year is eighth grade for you but, it's number twenty-five for me, and that . . . *is* significant. Do you know why, class?"

"Because it's your last?" Quinn blurted.

Without hesitating, she said, "Mr. Bates is correct! I'm in my final year. I figured twenty-five years of enlightening young minds was enough. So, to commemorate this momentous occasion, we will be sharing about our *extra special* summers one at a time. And I expect this will take, oh, I'm guessing, the entire first week. How does that sound?" she asked, looking down at her desk calendar.

No one moved, though a few still stared in Cade's direction.

"Great! This is always a treat for me, too." Her strained face tried to smile. "I want you to dig deep. What made this summer, well, summer to you? I won't take *No* for an answer. You have to say something, and I'd prefer if each of you could bring in something to show how break went. I won't take 'I watched TV' or 'Nothing' as an answer. I want PROOF!" She bellowed the last word from behind her desk, and crossed her arms militantly. Then, she started scribbling the order of presenters. Cade's name was written inside the second day of school. He didn't like it, but knew he couldn't argue with Ms.

Easter. She didn't budge on deadlines, he'd heard from upper-classmen. Especially since this was her last school year.

Quinn's name went down alongside his. The two fist bumped. Quinn tried to flirt with Valerie, and amazingly, thought Cade, she let him for a few brief seconds. Ms. Easter had to interrupt her long, laborious re-living of June and July to tell Quinsey to keep his hands to himself. "I won't tell you again," she ordered, her long, chicken-like neck strained.

"Ma'am?" he whined. "Valerie is hitting on *me*!"

Several of the boys laughed. Cade's ears went red at his friend's boldness.

"Mr. Bates, I have no qualms about calling your father and telling him about your behavior. Is that something you'd like?" she asked, as she resituated her flower-print dress and adjusted her thick glasses on a librarian's chain.

Quinn slumped in his chair, as Valerie giggled. "That goes for you too, Valerie, dearie," Ms. Easter scolded. "No way for a young lady to act."

Cade stared straight ahead at the board, barely listening to anything else said. He kept thinking about Crawford's pause at the mentioning of his dad - the *Explorer Extraordinaire*. Now, he rested somewhere salamanders swam. Cade shuddered at the slipperiness of the creature sitting in Crawford's desk, infrequently poking its head out to stare at the classroom.

Cade stood abruptly and scooted his chair into his desk. "I'm sorry, Ms. Easter. Really, I am," he said as he left the schoolhouse and headed home on his bike.

***

"You're an *Explorer* just like me," he heard in his sleep. He'd fallen into a fitful nap the moment he got home. It was the voice of his dad. Something Haven said to him every time they were about to go on an *Adventure*. It raised his spirits. Just like it always did. The words: Explorer and Adventurer were capitalized; they were proper nouns in his dad's voice. His words, whether from him or his memory, still held that power. It was like God let Cade re-experience him, beyond the cave of water holding him. When he woke, he felt like his dad was with him. He half expected to see him sitting at the foot of his bed.

Cade jumped up and ran to the shed. He stomped through the yard, feeling a pair of eyes on him. He turned suddenly to see Abbott Mize. "You know how to sneak up on people." Cade muttered, surprised.

"Plenty of practice living out here. Where were you traipsing to in such a hurry? You looked mighty determined."

"Just the shed. I left some stuff of Dad's. It's for school tomorrow," Cade said.

"What is it?"

Cade liked the lack of sensitivity about Abbott. He just said what he thought. No filter. "I'll show you. Hold on." Cade went into the shed and returned with the helmet, headlight, and welding rod. "These," he gestured, handing them over. "Underwater welding gear. It's for show-and-tell about our summers. Think it'll make for a good one?"

"I'm sure it will. Better to talk about it, too. Instead of keeping it all cooped up. Doesn't do a man much for keeping the truth buried. I should know." He spat tobacco leaves; something he seemed to constantly be chewing.

"What're you doing over here?"

Abbott shrugged his shoulders.

"Were we the first ones you told about your family leaving?"

"'Twas. I didn't expect to tell y'all, but you're such a talker. It came quite easy, I guess. And you know something? I realized it was silly to try and wrestle with it on my own like I had been. Guess that's why God put more than one person on this earth, huh?"

"Guess so," Cade agreed. He thought of life without his dad and mom. The thought triggered another shudder like he had when he saw the salamander at school. "I don't want to be alone like that ever."

"Well, you've got the opposite problem with me around. I'm not afraid of asking for your help. You should know that by now. Speaking of that . . . Listen, if you don't mind, could you leave your mom a note and come help me with some more fence posts? I've found that they won't dig themselves like I'd hoped." He laughed.

"Sure. She won't get home for a while. I'll write something and be right out."

"Here. Take these inside too. You don't want to lose these, before you get to talk about 'em tomorrow," Abbott said, handing Haven's gear back.

Cade said, "Thanks," and walked inside. Once he'd changed and written the note, he was inside the Ford pick-up truck and riding to the fence where he'd dug holes until his hands bled the week before. He was learning to both love and hate the same job; he didn't think that possible, but somehow, it was.

"We've done a lot, ain't we?" Cade beamed. "What ... another week and this thing will be licked?" he said. He realized he'd developed a lot of Abbottisms (which was what he was calling them) in the past few days.

"A week or two tops. Setting the posts, tamping 'em down, and pouring concrete is the easiest part," Abbott confirmed.

"What's this?" Cade asked, as the two stepped out of the truck and walked over to the edge of the yard—the entrance to their fence work. There were sawhorses with boards flayed across them, creating a platform. An extension cord ran from the rough-hewn barn walls to the contraption.

"Hold on," Abbott said and walked into the barn. He came out a moment later and held up a boom box like the ones Cade had seen in '90s movies. It was huge.

"Think this will draw in the bear?" Abbott joked. "If nothing else, it'll help us work." He plugged it in and found one of Seton's two radio stations: country or country.

Cade liked that Abbott opted for the older, twangy-sounding songs. It was the same with his dad, too. Abbott danced out to the soon-to-be dug hole and said, "Shall I, or you, young man?"

Cade extended his hand and accepted the post hold digger, the handle worn smooth from their previous efforts. He made a point to put the gloves on first and said, "Who sings this?"

"One of those Judds. I get 'em confused. Maybe Wynona. Which one was the actress?"

Cade didn't know what he was talking about. He shrugged. "It sounds good, whoever it is. Wish I could sing," he admitted. *I wish I could swim better, too. Things would be so different right now.*

Abbot interrupted him saying, "Anyone can sing. Just open your mouth and purr like a kitten. Some not as good as others though. Elvis was a rarity. He was the whole package. So was Reba. But, anyone can sing a lil bit. Just try," he prodded.

"Right now?" Cade said. "I thought we were building a fence."

"Building a fence and serenading the crickets," he added. "Give 'em a concert for a change. They're always playing their legs off for you, ain't they?"

Cade had never listened to the crickets long enough to know. He hardly knew Abbott, and here the old man wanted him to sing.

"I won't judge," Abbott said.

But, Cade couldn't get his vocal cords to cooperate.

Even when Abbott said, "Charley Pride. Sing this one on the radio." Cade had learned the chorus and opened his mouth. But, all he heard himself say, not sing, was something about kissing an angel and missing her, and the devil being in there somewhere. It was a tad confusing to him and he lost the song's lyrics in his mouth.

Abbott said, "No. Like this," and showed him his best Charley Pride sound. It was good, Cade admitted. Abbott's baritone voice boomed across the field, and even Clay perked his ears up in a friendly way.

Once the song ended, the two went back to talking about the fence. Cade saw headlights eventually at his house and knew his mom was home.

# CHAPTER EIGHT

All eyes were on Cade's back.

He picked up the chalk from the chalkboard tray and wrote, *My dad*. The chalk snapped in Cade's hand, and he picked up the broken pieces from the floor and put them into the tray. He turned to face the classroom.

Quinn grinned. He'd just delivered a goofy speech about the benefits of working at Mercer's Pub during summer.

Ms. Easter had asked, "Quinsey, what were you doing in a bar at thirteen years old? Don't your folks know it's against the law?"

Quinn shook his head. Argued that his uncle was Mercer, and he was his *understudy*. Claimed he was stock boy for all the liquors and such. The class applauded him, except for Cade—looking out the window.

"Well, at least you have some ambition. Albeit errant and haphazard," Ms. Easter added. "Cade, go ahead," she said, urging him to speak slowly. She wanted these presentations to save her from having to teach, he knew.

Cade looked at the three pieces of equipment on the table in front of him. He picked up the first, the helmet, and said flatly, "My summer was . . . the summer my dad disappeared."

All mouths were agape in the eighth grade room. The word *disappeared* freezing their attention and Quinn's grin falling flat.

"He was there one minute, and the next he wasn't. Like magic," Cade said.

Ms. Easter was noticeably disturbed, as she kept shifting her balance from elbow to elbow on the big, wooden teacher desk.

"Like a magic trick," Max said, shuffling his baseball cards without looking at them.

"He was there fishing and eating breakfast one minute, and then he went off on an *Adventure*." Cade made a point to grab the chalk piece again and wrote *Adventure* on the board but in cursive this time. He gripped it too tightly, and the chalk sounded like fingernails on the board—a few students grimaced.

"This Adventure was because he was an Explorer Extraordinaire like me," he said, pointing at his chest. "This helmet was for his skull. In case a cave wall or bridge pillar bumped against him underwater. It would protect his brain. And he wore it all the time." Cade fumbled for the next item. "This one, it's the second part of an explorer's gear, and Dad used it for lighting dark places. It's his headlight." He flashed the light on around the room for the class to see.

Mercedes McCall smiled, as Cade went over to hit the lights to show the class the brightness of his light, its settings.

"Oh, theatrics! How nice," Ms. Easter encouraged, trying to steady her voice, the topic obviously making her more nervous than it did anyone else.

"See, this light has three degrees of brightness. In a place like an underwater welder's office, you have to have a light that can reach the darkest spots just like a coal miner in a cave. Dad always said, 'Expect zero visibility down there. It gets cold and the pressure is there, too. Every day is different.' And, I imagine this light is what he's missing now that he's gone off on another Adventure. Don't you?"

Several heads nodded.

"And, this third piece of equipment is just as important as the other two. Can you see it?" He held the welding rod up for the middle school room.

"I can't see it," Quinn said. "Can I move up closer, Miss Easter?"

"Just for a moment," she said, relief in her voice. As she relinquished some of her control to Quinn, several hands shot up, and she instinctively said, "One at a time. You can come up and look at the pieces in single file."

"This one rod is part of the larger apparatus Dad uses to dive and repair bridges, dams, and other things. He used this very one to save thousands of lives downriver from Spoonbill Dam. You might've heard about it this past summer . . . his work, I mean. He was the reason Nashville didn't get flooded; he was fixing the dam."

A few of the students reached out for the welding rod, but Cade recoiled. "This one," he said, "you have to be very careful with. Because underwater welders have to watch out for different types of electrical currents when they're in the water. Dad always had to be careful using AC power. He'd be down there for as long as his diver's tank would allow, and his biggest enemy, he said, was electrocution. The electric was that important. He had to get it right," Cade added.

Ms. Easter was on her feet and thanking Cade for the astute synopsis of the welding profession. As Mercedes was helping him with the gear, most of the class was clapping and whistling at Cade. "Awesome!" Quinn yelled over the ruckus.

Then, Foster's hand shot into the air as the excitement died down. Foster was the class bully and had been for several years. Without waiting for Ms. Easter he blurted, "Well, if this *junk* is sooo important, and it's necessary for an adventure, why did your dad leave it all behind? That don't make no sense."

Cade didn't want to get into a fight, but he knew this was what Foster wanted. He had the strongest fists in middle school. "Like I said, he was in a hurry to get out and *Explore*! other parts of the world. He'll come back when he's good and ready, Foster." He hoped this was true. Maybe it was why he hadn't really cried that much for Dad.

"I think you know that's a bunch of bull," Foster egged. "Just like you moving away from Cumberland Lake. My dad said your dad drowned. They just ain't found the body yet. You don't plan on living there ever again, do you? It's because of what happened at Spoonbill. I knew it! It's haunted! I knew it! I knew it!"

Ms. Easter grabbed him and sat him down hard in his chair. "Ouch!" he bellowed. "I'll have you put in the slammer, old bird! Your last year and all. What a shame that'd be to lose your retirement."

"You'll apologize for what you said, and you'll do it now. Or we'll wait until the end of the day to move on," she said flatly.

"Well, he *is* gone. We all know that. Why do we have to lie? It's not a big adventure or any of that junk. He's just *dead*."

The class gasped collectively, and Mercedes reached for Cade's hand, but he denied her. He scooped up his dad's gear and tucked it into his duffelbag.

Cade grabbed his dad's gear and bolted for the second day in a row and biked toward the outskirts of town. He wondered if he'd make it to high school or quit before he got there. At this rate, he didn't care. *Dad, you're not dead, are you? Please come back.*

Tears streamed down Cade's face by the time he'd reached the front porch. This time, Abbott wasn't there. He didn't need him either. Just a bum hanging onto the same hope as him. Hoping someone would come back that wouldn't ever.

Cade pitched himself onto his stiff mattress, and fell asleep, not caring about anything at all, least of all his eighth grade classmates.

# CHAPTER NINE

He woke to a faint knocking on the bedroom door.

"Honey? Honey? Can we bother you a minute?"

Cade rubbed his red eyes and rolled over. "We?" he asked. "I don't want to see anyon—"

He paused, as Mercedes appeared behind his mom.

"Cade," she said, stepping over to his bedside, as if her being there wasn't unusual at all. Her frizzy, brown hair shook in front of her eyes, and she swiped it back, tucking it unsuccessfully behind her ears. She laughed at the hassle and bit her fingernail.

"What're you doing here?" he asked, instinctively pushing his messed up hair down. Her presence made him giddy, even when he was mad. "Foster doesn't know—"

"A thing. I know. I hope he learns that before it's too late," she confirmed. "He's as enlightened as a bulldog."

"What're you doing here?" he asked again, aware of her scent – a fresh linens and peach concoction.

"I just wanted to check on you."

Mercedes sat down on his Wolverine comforter and rubbed her hand over the X-Men emblem like she expected the inanimate object to cooperate. Cade marveled at the female instinct to soothe. He reached out and grabbed her tender hand.

"I'm fine," he told her. "Honestly. I don't need any babying or anything. I left, because—"

"Because Foster's a jerk," she said. "He is. Your dad could be in China for all we know," she added.

Mercedes' rescue was welcome. He'd always had a crush on her; she always made him blush. Cade thought about holding her hand as his mom brought in a bowl of reheated chicken broth. "Thanks, Mom," he said.

"I'm here if you need anything else, baby," his mom said.

Cade winced at the label and waved her away.

"What do you plan to do tomorrow?" Mercedes asked, her sandy brown hair falling over her shoulders, as she moved closer. "Are you going to stand up to Foster?"

"I'd like to," Cade feebly agreed, forgetting that he'd have to go back. "How many days can a person miss, before they flunk eighth grade?"

Mercedes shrugged; she looked out his bedroom window.

"Let's get out of here," Cade encouraged, afraid for her to see him weaker than he already was.

"And do what?"

"Let's go for a walk. I need to clear my head."

"Have you not checked out what's in this field yet?"

"Naw. I've been too busy building Abbott Mize's fence over there." He pointed, and she squinted at the farm in the distance.

"All this time?"

"It's only been a few weeks. Besides, it's a pretty big fence. I'll show you sometime."

She gave a noncommittal nod and looked back to the Rainy acreage. "Let's check it out!"

Her excitement caught Cade off-guard, and he was suddenly motivated to see the farmland and pasture, too. He knew the fifty acres would probably only be fescue grass, clover, and rocks strewn about, but he kept his hopes up. At least he would get to walk around with her.

The two strolled down the hill behind the ranch home and out the first gate that separated them from the tall grass. There, Mercedes pointed out a type of bird Cade had never paid attention to. She said, "Barn swallow," as it swooped past their heads and flew low, driving arcs around the grass. The bird didn't seem the least bit perturbed by them. "They like barns, and they're very resourceful," she recited, like she'd read it from a biology book.

"There's a barn at Abbott's. They could be nesting over there."

"Probably. Have you heard baby birds chirping?"

Cade shook his head. He'd been too focused on building things with Mize. He didn't think he'd heard a chirp or anything from the barn.

"It's okay. They're friendly," Mercedes said, in a light, tender voice. Her tanned arms reached to hug Cade. When she grasped him, she brought a warmth he didn't expect. Her slight sweat made him aware of her closeness. It was the closest to a girl he had ever been. He looked to the house and expected his mom to walk out any moment.

"Let's check out the fields," he heard himself say in a contented voice, stronger than he knew he possessed.

Mercedes let him lead the way. And they tramped past the first field into the second, around an abandoned watering trough and ring pen for breaking wild stallions.

Cade and Mercedes went to the backside of the hill, where a dried-out pond lay exhausted—an unchecked leak having rendered it useless.

"Too dry even for turtles," she said.

"Do you think the fish all suffocated?" Cade asked, fear showing in his eyes.

Seeing the look, Mercedes replied, "They found their way out."

"So they're safe, ya think?"

"Of course. God looks after all of them. All the time. You know?"

He wanted to believe her, as her sandy hair tossed and her soft hand held his. Cade cleared his throat. "Let's check back there."

"Lead the way," she said. Her voice was genuinely engaged, flirty even, Cade felt.

The two kept walking, high-stepping the chiggers and ticks along the overgrown path.

***

It was covered by the kudzu and ivy: an opening into the earth and beyond.

Cade and Mercedes saw the pesky vines and didn't think anything of it at first. They just heard the water trickling down from the greenery and felt thirst. But a closer look showed a dark recess. Cade held the kudzu back and peered into the expansive darkness. His first thought was a fear of falling. The drop off beyond the mouth looked monumental. Mercedes held onto his other arm, begging him to be careful.

"We have a place to explore, M!" he said loudly. Shocked he'd given her a nickname in the process.

Cade looked into the darkness and gazed back at her soft green eyes, her button nose. She looked like a modern-day Pocahontas. Her gaze was uniquely her own, though, and it was affectionate like no one else he knew. Did she like him like that? He didn't know, but he told her it would be all right, as they entered the cave.

Inside the cave, it was *dark*. Cade couldn't see much, and Mercedes kept bumping into him. He feigned bravery. The disorientation continued for a few minutes, until their pupils adjusted to the dimness.

Cade thought about the sci-fi movie *Avatar*—how otherworldly space could feel. Except instead of Jake Sully infiltrating the Na'vi people and trying to rid them of their precious materials, Cade was trying to act strong inside a cave with a girl he wanted to know better. Mercedes didn't let any fear show, if it was there at all. She held Cade's hand firmly and followed along.

Cade treaded through the first two hundred yards of the cave's descent slowly. His footing was uncertain at each step—and as the space darkened, the farther they went—he made sure to take care of her. He kept saying things like *Watch your head.* She didn't seem to mind the instructions, because her grip never slackened.

Then, the noises came loudly from the darkness ahead.

"What is that?" she asked with a tremble to her voice.

Cade thought it was bats, and he was right. The faint chirping became an extra-loud squawk in a matter of seconds. *There were hundreds of them!* They traveled up the incline the two had just traversed and flew into the early evening brightness. "Check it out!"

"I thought they only came out at night?" Mercedes laughed.

"Me, too. I guess we disturbed 'em," Cade said. "It looks like the cave keeps going." He exhaled, gesturing to the darkness ahead.

"We could go farther," Mercedes said, holding Cade's arm the tightest she had all day.

He read into that sentiment. But, the trip needed more preparation. More equipment. Suddenly, he thought of his dad's gear.

"I got it!" he shouted, his voice echoing around the blind cave, scaring Mercedes, her hands tightening around his bicep.

"Are you trying to make me pee myself?"

"I'm sorry. No. I just thought of something that'll help. It can help us *Explore* this cave," he added. "It can be our secret."

Mercedes must've liked the idea, because she gripped him tighter. Her perfume was sweet-smelling and it met his nose in just the right way. Cade waited for her to speak in her soft voice, but she didn't.

"Tomorrow," his voice offered. "After school. We'll come back to the cave and bring gear with us. That way, we'll be able to search it proper."

She pecked his cheek, and Cade lost his breath. His legs grew weary, and she steadied him with her arms locked inside one of his. She asked if his dad taught him a lot about being brave.

Cade remembered the fly fishing, the hard work. Finally, he said, "Dad taught me a little bit about everything. I guess he's still teaching me."

The two exited the cave and crossed the field. Mercedes said bye, and went to the edge of the driveway, where her mom was in their family minivan—waiting to pick her up. She waved and blew him a kiss.

Cade didn't want to look silly, but if his mom, who was standing inside their doorway watching, saw him blush, she didn't say so. All she said was, "Dinner's almost ready" and held the door ajar. Then added, "She's sweet."

He didn't confirm or deny it. There was a cave behind his house, and Mercedes' scent clung to him like nothing else.

# CHAPTER TEN

Mercedes and Cade exchanged glances during Ms. Easter's lessons on quadratic equations and Punnett squares. Math and science couldn't hold their attention. The cave awaited.

Quinsey hit Cade in the back of the head. *Smack!* The clock ticked slowly. It seemed to be moving backward somehow.

When he took the fourth hit, Cade turned and rubbed the throbbing welt. "Would you just stop?!"

"Don't fence me out, bro," Quinn's deeper voice growled. "You know I hate that."

Cade despised how even his best friend's angry voice was still persuasive. "Listen, I'm not trying to," his eyes moving to Mercedes' curls.

"I see. I see it. Right there," Quinn grunted. "Girlfriend replaces best friend. Am I right?"

Ms. Easter paused mid-equation and looked at the disruption. She had little patience for hijinks. Her eyes roved over the two, lingered for an uncomfortable second, and then darted back to the board.

"Okay, man. I like her," Cade mumbled out of the corner of his mouth. "She's hot," he said. "And there's something else . . ."

The way he said it must have impacted his usually unimpressed friend, because Quinn leaned back, eyebrows raised. He did something he never did and wrote a note. The words sailed to Cade via paper: *Better be straight with me after school.*

Cade crumpled the note and gave one quick nod to confirm. He tossed the paper at the basket and missed.

Ms. Easter didn't notice, as her back was still turned, "Quadratic equations are the friends of factoring . . . factoring and squares just like the squares in biology class. You know, Punnett squares . . . get it?"

No one chimed in, as she went on with her chalkboard pecking. Mercedes normally answered every question, but it was obvious she was excited about the cave, too, as her eyes kept shifting between her cell and Cade.

The lunch bell struck them all awake, and thirty-five students exited the room. Ms. Easter never halted in her spiel, even as the room emptied. The three explorers were the last to leave, and Quinn gave Mercedes a knowing look.

"You told *him*?" she asked Cade, walking down the hall. The smell of beefaroni was prominent to Cade's nose. Not beefaroni again, he thought.

"Why wouldn't he tell me, sis?" Quinn teased. "I've been his friend longer than you've been getting perms."

Mercedes crossed her arms and tried to act unhurt by his words.

"I didn't tell him, but I should because he's legit. You can trust him to keep *our* secret," Cade urged. "Honest."

She didn't unfold her arms until grabbing a tray with some milk and fruit, and they sat down at a table in the back of the lunchroom.

Cade was right about the beefaroni, and he hated being right. It smelled bad and tasted worse. He prayed they'd added cheese since the last time, but the cheese was still missing. It was an odd mixture of marinara sauce, undercooked elbow noodles, and zero salt. Too minimal to resemble lasagna and too intentional to be anything other than an underfunded Kentucky lunchroom's attempt at Italian cuisine. Cade cleared his throat. "Here goes nothing," he said scooping a fork full.

The two watched him force it. Cade's stomach growled with reproach, but he held the entrée down.

Quinn drummed his fingers on the pressboard table surface. "So what'd you find, Dora the Explorer?"

Cade swallowed more rubbery noodles and took a swig of the ice cold 2% milk to wash it down. He looked over and saw Mercedes waiting for him to say something first.

"I . . . me and M found something behind my house."

"Your old house? The lake house? I thought you weren't going back there anymore since the—"

"Not there, dummy. My new one. The ranch house. Out behind it in the acreage. We went back there just walking and came across an opening," he said, his voice rising.

"Walking? Just walking, huh?" Quinn pried.

"You're not listening," Mercedes said, trying to keep the topic away from Quinn's girl-crazy brain. "Tell him, Cade."

The way she said his name was elongated like the way Abbott did, but the *Cayd* had a purr to it almost. It made him lose focus. His friend tapped his shoulder.

"Right. We were walking, and there was a hidden entrance behind some kudzu and ivy. Guess what it was?" Cade asked, unaware that he was gripping Quinn's arm.

"I don't know, but if you don't let go of me, I'm going to show you stars, man."

Cade let go, and said, "A cave," with as much conviction as he could – for him, a clear call to action.

The words hung in the stuffy, lunchroom air amid the chatter of music and middle school drama.

"A cave? In your backyard?" Quinn corrected, aware of Cade's gaze.

"That's right! Just sitting back there waiting for *us*," he said, aware his secret with M had lost its privacy somewhat. "Do you want to go with us, man?"

Quinn leaned back and inspected his milk carton. Cade saw him reading the corny anecdotes they put on the side of the part-paper, part-plastic label. It was always something like "Drink milk, grow muscles" or "Stay awake with Vitamin D." Cade always appreciated the effort some designer somewhere put into this little extra touch. Today, Quinn just crumpled his carton and tossed it onto the tray. "I guess I'll go spelunking with you kids. Someone has to keep an eye on you, in case you run into cave dwellers." He grinned.

Cade exhaled, happy with his friend. He noticed M looking rigid like she'd been stranded on the tilt-a-whirl or something. She said, "Troglodytes," and closed her lips.

"Huh?" Quinn grunted.

"Trog—"

"I heard you," he interrupted. "But what's that big word mean?"

"Cave dwellers, dummy."

"I knew that," he puffed up.

"I'll take care of you, M," Cade soothed, rubbing her elbow. "It's settled then. Back to my place, and we'll explore. I've got the gear already set up."

"Won't your mom wonder where you are? I mean, if it takes us a while to find where we're going down there?" Mercedes pointed below the table to the tiled, cafeteria flooring.

Quinn smiled. "Can't wait, buddy! I can go home and get a light, too."

"We don't have that much time. You're all the way down at Cumberland almost. I've made up a note that's already on my kitchen table at home," Cade said, turning to Mercedes. "Mom'll be happy we're outside and not moping around."

"Okay," she said, her face brightening somewhat.

The lunchroom bell buzzed, and the teens stood. Cade was happy lunch was over, but even happier his best friend and new girl agreed on something. Then, it was P.E., and then classes let out. He didn't know how, but he felt the day would get even better. And the excitement made him nervous.

***

The headlight worked magnificently. It cast a nice strong glow across the chasm as the trio made their descent into the cave's first large room—the one Mercedes and he first saw. He remembered the light had three levels of intensity, and he turned it on to its highest strength and placed the elastic band around his helmet. It was a bit too large for his head, and the size made him suddenly remember how his dad wore it.

On instinct, Mercedes gripped his arm and marched alongside him step by step. Quinn hung back, but not too far.

"It's so much cooler right here," she whispered, her voice still echoing around the walls.

Cade looked for the bats and wondered how many were sleeping upside down. He was an *Explorer* in this moment; he felt like his dad. Except he'd left the welding rod behind, and there wasn't water where they were now.

Quinn motioned toward a fork in the cave and said, "Have you been through there?"

"This is as far as we've been. You could say this is the threshold, man," Cade beamed, happy to have this moment with his friends, especially M.

Cade waited for Quinn to make some reference to their favorite movies. He was sure *Lord of the Rings* was about to be quoted, probably the part where Samwise Gamgee mentioned it was the farthest he'd been from home. But, he didn't. Quinn kept looking left and then right. Cade had never seen his friend so quiet before. Yet, this was uncharted territory for all of them.

"To boldly go," M suddenly said, and the boys' heads snapped in her direction.

"You speak Star Trek?" Cade asked.

"She's just messin' with us," Quinn said.

"No. I've seen the show. I like the newer movies better though," she admitted. "Chris Pine's pretty hot."

"I brought this in case we got stuck," Cade said, retrieving a Zippo from his cargo shorts, changing the topic. "Just like the movies. Follow the air, right? That'll lead us to a path that rejoins the surface," he said, trying to sound smart, remembering a scene from *Rambo First Blood*.

"Lead on, Cade," Quinn said. "She's too busy thinking about Captain Kirk over here."

Cade started to push his friend, but Mercedes grabbed his elbow again, and he halted. "Don't worry. Chris Pine is just a phony. You're real, and I know the difference," she said. Her words made him lose focus a little bit. "I trust you'll see us through."

Cade pointed to the left where the Zippo flame had flickered in his hand. All three maneuvered single file down the corridor, as the tunnel became more and more narrow. Mercedes' breathing quickened behind Cade. She said she had a slight case of claustrophobia.

"Slow and steady," Quinn said behind her. "We'll all three get where we're going, if nobody freaks out. Okay?"

Mercedes nodded her head, but neither could see her in the darkness. Cade's headlight was pointed straight ahead, and the tunnel's narrowness and dampness started to become really irksome. Eventually, Mercedes tugged on Cade's shirt a little. "When you get a chance, let's hold up and rest for a second."

Cade understood her fear, her small voice. The tunnel looked oppressive from his firsthand account at the front of the line. He saw a smaller and smaller hole that looked as if it might require stooping, and eventually, crawling before they'd reach the next larger chamber. Up ahead, he heard a sound, and he didn't know if he could press on or not. It triggered a memory, a flash. Suddenly, he was back at Spoonbill Dam. His dad was going to check on the dam's leak. Then, he remembered waking up and learning of his dad's disappearance—the water everywhere. Cade's fear of not being able to swim, and still stronger desire to jump into the abysmal water, haunted him. He gripped the cave walls, his hands recoiling at their slimy slipperiness. They were still in the tight, close quarters of the cave.

"It's okay, man! It's okay. Let's just move slowly to the next opening," Quinn said, pointing to an area fifty yards ahead.

Cade saw the opening but also saw the wet, jagged rocks that would make them stoop, and crawl the last leg of this corridor. The *whooshing* sound was water, and it was traveling fast from somewhere. Cade breathed deeply and exhaled. *I didn't know there was water.* He tried to steady himself, as he looked into Mercedes' green eyes.

She squeezed his hand to signify she was ready and trusted him.

Cade stooped and wiggled through the maze of boulders and waited for his companions to catch up. When both looked ready, eager even, to see the opening, Cade pushed through the crevice and helped Mercedes stand. All three turned and saw water and movement everywhere around them.

***

The subterranean water flow was expansive and loud. Cade scanned his light over it, and he felt a chill in his bones. *Is this the same water Dad last entered?* But, he quickly shook the thought away, as Mercedes and Quinn were loping toward the water and hooting like mad children. He wanted to run with them, but he realized he was going at a much slower pace.

The rocks *were* slippery, and he thought he saw some brown bats hanging upside down above him. Mercedes did something unexpected and jumped into the water. Cade yelling after her, "No! M, what're you doing?!" But, his voice was indiscernible in the midst of the roaring water.

"Just let her go, man," Quinn said, as he threw his shirt off and dove into the water as well.

Cade didn't like his friend's tone, and he especially didn't like him jumping into the murkiness with M. Cade watched as both swam underwater. The absence of them—alone, reminiscent of the summer's end—made him want to run back toward the tight corridor, any exit he could find. Then M came up for air.

"It's fr-freezing!"

Quinn burst to the surface of the pool. "It couldn't be over forty degrees," he shouted as he spat water at Cade.

He wanted to scold Quinn and ignore Mercedes, at least, until they were back on the rocks. And it didn't take long. The chill from the air made them rejoin him in an instant.

"That might've been the dumbest thing I've ever done," Mercedes laughed, as she tried to fling water off of herself.

Cade admired her energy, even though he felt left out.

"Did you feel something brush your leg down there?" Quinn asked her, teeth chattering.

Her bottom lip quivered, as her smile went away. She shook her head.

"Nothing at all?" he asked. "Well, I did. I felt scales or something. And, I could've sworn it moved right past me like I was just another bit of debris."

Mercedes stared, and Cade pushed Quinn's arm. "Quit messing with her."

"I'm not. There're fish down there. How? I don't know. But, they're there all right. Trust me."

M clung to Cade's arm, and her dripping wetness made him cold, too. He thought about recoiling but didn't.

"Aren't you glad you came?" Cade heard himself say.

"Darn straight. Samwise Gamgee wouldn't miss this for the world," Quinn said, punching his friend's arm. "Aren't you going to get hypothermia with us?"

Cade ignored the question and scanned the cave with his light. He didn't see any bats, but he thought he heard another sound. He tried to place it. The sound came across whispery and faint, and he thought it might've been Mercedes whispering to him, but it wasn't. Her lips were chattering from the cold water, which clung to her clothes, her curvy body.

Quinn said, "What're you doing?"

"You don't hear that?"

"The sound of my teeth knocking together is all I hear, buddy!"

"No. Something else. It's low and hollow sounding."

"You're acting a bit cuckoo. Maybe you need to get back to the surface. Get some O2."

"I'm fine. But one thing's for sure. I don't plan on jumping into that water. Not unless you throw me, and I wouldn't recommend it. I might drag you with me," Cade said.

Seton Middle felt forever away. Cade didn't know how a cave could provide such distance, but it did. Apart from the cold, rushing, life-threatening water, it was a new world he wanted to search and *Invade*. The word hit him like a rock, and he didn't know why he thought of invading a blank, dark void. Maybe it was his way of rectifying his dad's departure? Staking claim in an uncharted world or something? But either way, it was a place he didn't want to leave. And the moment he thought this, his cave light flickered on and off and back on again.

"Uh oh," Quinn teased.

"I think we'd be okay for a little bit longer, but maybe we shouldn't take any chances. Not today," Mercedes said.

The two boys waited a moment, wanting to see which would make for home first. Cade stared at Quinn and his light flickered again.

"I'll lead if neither of you will," she said, fear surfacing in her voice.

"If we go back the way we came, at least we know how long it'll be," Cade said.

"Or, we could go this way and follow the wind tunnel?" Quinn countered.

"And how long would that take do you think? You've seen *The Descent*, remember? Those girls didn't fare so well, did they?"

"Hollywood," Quinn argued. "They always show the worst-case scenario. I mean, British girls in Appalachia, gettin' eaten by critters that look like Gollum. Blind and everything. C'mon!"

"I didn't say it was accurate, but at least we know there's a way back the direction we came," Cade said.

Mercedes' teeth were chattering loud enough to hear above the other noises now, and Cade shone his light on her. He held her shoulders and tried to soothe her. "That's enough of the Gollum talk, please," she said.

"It's okay. We'll go back the way we came, and I'll have you back with the living in no time," Cade encouraged. "This way. Everyone breathe in and get ready for the squeeze," as he hiked up a pant leg and turned.

Quinn looked behind them and toward the direction the water flowed. "Are you sure you don't want to chance it?"

"We'll get it next time. At least we know there's another entry point. We can follow it all the way and then map it from the outside as well," Cade said.

Quinn, obviously satisfied with this idea, turned around and followed the meandering tunnel and his friends.

Mercedes' feet were so close to Cade's that she stepped on his heels more than once—his Chuck Taylor's slipping off his heels each time. Rather than scolding her, he just paused and said, "No sweat," each time.

When they arrived at the first large chamber, the cave light went out completely, and Cade momentarily lost his bearing in the titanic room. He heard, "Are we lost?" from Quinn, and "Don't leave me!" from M.

Cade assured both that their trajectory was pretty straightforward into and out of the cave's main entrance. "Even if we got lost here, it's just a little blip, because there's only the way we came in. As long as we don't turn all the way around and go *downhill* again, we'll climb out eventually."

This answer seemed to assuage both friends, because they waited for him to move forward. Without the light, it was extremely difficult to see the mouth of the cave. Only a tiny speck of light led them from above. Cade took his time and waited periodically for them to catch up. The main room was so broad that when they closed in on the light, Cade saw that Quinn was actually side-by-side with him. "Wait up!" he heard Mercedes shout, her voice echoing around the room.

"We're right here, M. Nobody's leaving you, not even Quinn," Cade said, as his friend elbowed him.

In their climb up the final steep hill, she missed a foothold and slipped on a wet rock. Cade caught her before she fell backward, and he could smell her sweet perfume.

"Thanks for saving me."

Quinn moved past them, as they exited the cave's mouth, and he jumped up and down in the sunlight doing his best dance. "Can you believe it's still this light out?" he said. "It looked like midnight down there, and I expected it to be, but it's not."

"Just like outer space," M rejoined. "Maybe time slows down when you go into a cave like it does on Star Trek when they go to warp speed?"

Cade looked at her in the bright, illuminated afternoon sun, and found himself staring longer than he meant to. She was the most amazing girl he'd ever met.

"Pick the drool up off of your chin," Quinn teased. "She's gonna call the cops if you keep staring, man!"

Cade checked his lip absentmindedly for drool and realized Quinn was just messing. Mercedes giggled and tried to wring her shirt dry. The dampness clung to her clothes.

"I feel great, but I didn't jump into that frigid water like you two idiots," Cade said.

"Yeah, why didn't you?" Quinn asked absentmindedly.

Mercedes hit him in the gut. "He's been through hell this past summer, dummy."

"It's okay," Cade said, waving her off.

"My bad, bro. You know I didn't mean to—"

"I said it's fine. I need to learn to get past my fear anyways. At least I can still get in the shower without going berserk, right?" Cade tried to joke.

Neither laughed.

"C'mon. I'm okay. Honest. Or at least better than I was. Seeing you two jump into that forty-degree pool helped me. Swear."

Quinn play-punched him, but Mercedes just stared—worry on her face.

"Promise. Being around it will be the best cure. Mom thought moving away from the lake was the answer, but I know facing my fears head-on will be better. Thanks for going, Quinn. And, M … thanks for going back."

"I'd do it again tonight, if you wanted to," she said.

"I'll get more batteries for the light, and I'll try to get one for each of us. We might have to take a few days off, but we'll explore it all. Quinn, do you have any allowance money to put toward the cause?"

"Tomorrow at lunch," he said. "I'll hook you up."

"Sounds good," Cade said.

"Well, if that's the end of our first expedition, I'm going to let you two love bugs spend some alone time together, and I'll see you at Seton tomorrow. Good?"

"Good," Cade said, a little too quickly.

"Easy, killer," Quinn teased.

M laughed, both at the abruptness in Cade's voice and Quinn's joke.

The three stood in silence for another minute, and suddenly, Quinn turned, jogged to his bike and pedaled down the road—toward town. Mercedes looked at Cade. Then she hugged him unexpectedly. "You were brave today," she said.

"Thanks," Cade laughed.

"I mean it," she countered. "It takes a lot to go into a cave. Takes guts," her sweet voice urged.

This time Cade hugged her and didn't mind the water from her clothes soaking him.

"Thanks, I think," she kidded back. "You're not too bad at that."

"Hugging?" he asked.

"That *and* exploring," she said. "If that was your first expedition, I would let you lead anytime."

"I guess I'll have to keep that in mind." A wry smile played across his lips.

"You had to go and make it creepy, didn't you?" she laughed.

"I guess I get it from Quinn," Cade said.

"He's a bad influence."

The two walked back toward the ranch home, where light shone inside the kitchen. When they entered, they saw his mom fixing supper, and the smell of fried chicken and peach cobbler wafted down the hallway. Sitting at the table was Abbott Mize, who stood to greet them.

Cade tried to wipe his dirty, muddied cave gunk on the floor mat. "This is Mercedes McCall. She's my—we're classmates at Seton Middle," he corrected, blushing.

His mom stifled a laugh, as Abbott held out his hand. "Abbott Mize. Abbott's fine, or Mize. Whichever one. Pleased to meet you, miss."

"Likewise," Mercedes said.

His mom held her hand out at the same time, and she shook Mercedes' hand saying, "Mrs. Hollie Rainy." There was a pause after.

"Mercedes McCall," Mercedes said, and this broke the tension a little, because his mom laughed.

"Of course you are," she said. "So glad you joined us. Cade, please show our guest where the washroom is, and you two wash up before we dig in, okay? And Cade, be sure to take those shoes off. They're filthy."

"Yes, ma'am," he answered. "We'll be right back."

And they were. The smell was so intoxicating that there was little said for several minutes, except for grace. The chicken livers went quickly. Cade tried to use his napkin and not chew with his mouth open while Mercedes was there.

"So, I've been meaning to ask why your shoes look the way they do, pardner," Abbott said, breaking the silence and pointing to the muddiness on the floor.

Cade looked down and then glanced at M. Her eyes fell away from his. "I guess you could say it was—"

"We found a mud hole in the back of the field," Mercedes said flatly.

Cade didn't know what to think. Had she just helped him protect their secret? Was it a lie? He shook his head, and heard himself add, "A great big one! It was a lot of fun. M is soaking wet."

Hollie reached out and felt Mercedes' clothing, which had dried a little. She said, "My, she is! Good grief, child. You need to get out of those or you'll get pneumonia for sure. Here, let me go get you something dry. I might have something that would fit you. Okay?"

"No. It's fine. I'm drying off fine. Don't bother yourself," Mercedes tried to say, but Hollie was already gone to the other room.

"Mud hole, huh?" Abbott surmised. "Must've been one of those hidden ones there in the back of the field. Way back . . ."

Cade saw his eyes, a twinkle in them. Then, the old man laughed and didn't try to stifle it.

Hollie reappeared with a shirt and a worn pair of jean shorts. She handed them to M and said, "Here, try these on. Go change in the washroom." And, she turned to Abbott, "What's so funny that's got you shaking the walls, Abbott Mize?"

"Oh, nothing worth repeating," he said, winking at Cade and Mercedes. "It just seems your boy and his classmate found a new place in the back of your field. Now, if I could just get him *that* excited about building fences and breaking geldings, I'd be set."

He looked at Cade and gave him a knowing look. The boy watched Mercedes stand up to go change, and he thought of the wild sounds he'd heard inside the cave just hours ago.

# CHAPTER ELEVEN

Four years later

The decrepit, weathered brick building of the Bigsby Food Market was not his dream job.

Cade—now taller than his dad had been, with a short, bristly beard—knew it when he took the apron and agreed to stock shelves the beginning of his senior year. But, he'd plugged along from fall to spring, and his company-provided, back brace had seen a lot of use. The resistant tug when he'd picked up a heavy box of canned green beans in October—the weight ripping the box apart, sending cans everywhere—still unnerved him and it was now June. The high school graduate made a point to lift with his legs the next time. His manager, Mr. Bill Clip, was always close on his heels, ready to strike.

Cade chuckled at the man's name. *Bill Clip.* Who was named that anyway? The joke had been fresher when the skinny, five-foot six-inch man first held out his hand and said, "Bill Clip" in a high-pitched, nasally tone.

Cade did a double-take, offered his hand, and stifled his first (of many) immature laughs. Now, when he saw the skinny man approaching, he knew it went beyond a joke. Everything had grown weary within him. Bill looked tired, too. His appearance was unkempt since the start of spring, and he was slipping in his managerial duties—forgetting to nag Cade every chance he got.

Just yesterday, Cade had turned the Swiss Cake Rolls upside down and backward in their rows at the checkout, to see if Mr. Clip would notice.

He did not.

His nose was constantly red, and he always looked like he might bump into somebody and topple over.

Just as he was thinking of Bill Clip and placing Cheetos in their respective Aisle 14, or, what Mercedes called, "The Unhealthy Aisle," the weakened manager appeared.

"Cade, did you find a place for all those stickers on Bolthouse markdowns earlier?" Clip asked, stifling a sneeze.

"I did, sir," Cade said, trying to be respectful, unsure of why he was still trying at all. Mercedes had left for summer – equine camp.

"Well, some of them are missing their red stickers. I just checked. Again, if you can't make this work, I'm going to have to find somebody else. There're plenty of kids needing summer jobs. Seton might be small, but I can find someone who needs work," he threatened, eyes bloodshot.

"You don't look so well," Cade said. "Can I get you something?"

"Markdowns!" Bill Clip said, stomping his foot. The small shoe made a slight noise on the tile. "Hop to it, Rainy! Have them done before your break."

"Got it, Mr. Clip," Cade said, no longer curious about what was making Clip fall apart the way he was. He just wanted to get away from the Bigsby Market as quickly as he could.

But then, a customer tapped him on the shoulder. "Paper plates? We're having a picnic down at Cumberland. What aisle for plates?" the lady asked, looking for his nametag.

The mention of the lake unnerved him even four years later. He fumbled with the box cutter, and set it down with a clank. "Plates? Plates. Yes. Aisle 13. One over from "The Unhealth—, um, this aisle," he caught himself. "One aisle over," he pointed to his left.

The customer followed his finger. "Thanks."

Cade picked up the box cutter and sliced through the box and retrieved what felt like an endless amount of cheese puffs. He stocked the shelves until they were at capacity. How could Cheetos be so innumerable? Did everyone but his family eat them?

Finally, he stood and walked over to the juice aisle, or Mercedes' "Healthy Aisle 1." Cade picked up a magazine called, *You Weekly*, and it had pictures of every star and celebrity he'd ever heard of, and several he couldn't name. The magazine showcased many attractive faces on the cover. It was crazy how many faces were plastered across it. So many beautiful people, and all of them seemed to know where they were going. He was tired of Seton and tired of the 581 people who lived there—according to the city limit sign. *Did that count Dad or not?* Cade shook his head and thought of M going to the University of Kentucky. Quinn had even signed up to go to college. He was going to Western Kentucky University in Bowling Green. The image of his best friend and girlfriend traveling away, even just two hours, didn't seem fair. But, he remembered, their families had set aside money specifically for college.

The Bolthouse juice was always going on markdown, because it was considered fresh. *It,* unlike most items in the Bigsby Food Market, had an expiration date. Cade picked up a carrot juice bottle and it read one day away from certain death. Cade set it down and located his markdown gun—his favorite part of the job, apart from harassing Bill Clip. He spun the gauge around to the proper read out: 0.99 and snapped the red stickers onto every bottle.

Cade placed the markdown gun in his apron. Before he walked away, he picked the gun back out of his cotton apron and blew on the gun like he was in a Western. It made him feel better. Quinn would've appreciated the sentiment.

As he rounded Aisle 1, he came to the seafood counter, or what barely constituted one. Cade knew Seton, Kentucky was landlocked, but did it have to be so poor in every respect, including fish reserves? *There's a lake right over there,* he wanted to shout at customers. *Someone go grab a rod and reel and get busy!* But, he never said this. Mr. Clip didn't give him much time to daydream either. Even with his runny nose and bloodshot eyes, he was still alert enough to keep Cade moving.

Just then, Cade heard, "Finished, Rainy?"

Cade turned and saw the bloodhound hot on his heels. "Yes, sir!"

"Good. Good man. Now, if you'll clean up the spill at the lobster tank, before a customer slips and falls and we have a lawsuit on our hands," Mr. Clip wheezed.

"Got it! Where are the—"

"Where they always are! Do I have to reteach you every time?"

"No, sir," and Cade was behind the butcher's wall, hunting for the mop—an item always on the move.

To his amazement, he found the mop and its roller-bucket right where he'd last spotted it. Instinctively, Cade filled the bucket with warm water and soap, and rolled it out onto the main floor. He parked it beside the sorry excuse for a lobster tank, holding one aging lobster that'd been in the tank—staring, ogling at Cade—for months.

"It's me or you, buddy," Cade said. "Money's on me going first. People in this town don't have a lobster budget. You might be the only lobster to ever die of old age."

The lobster moved his pinchers back and forth and snapped the dirty, brownish water. The rubber bands holding his claws shut had long since eroded and fallen away. His lack of competition never required them to be re-shut, and the water had stopped being changed—due to his permanent stay. Cade despised the lobster, but even more, his habitat; the murky water sloshing back and forth, and the air bubbles churning the filth around and around the enclosed space.

The moving water made Cade think of Spoonbill. He didn't know why. The floodgates—a sight he hadn't seen in over four years. More than likely, it was the color of the water. Brown, gritty and resembling the cascading image after the blue, green pool joined the bottom of Cumberland Lake. The falls made the water bubble and fester and turn a new, less attractive, rust color. Sickly.

Cade started mopping around the tank. The tank had leaked non-stop since Cade started at the Bigsby. Grabbing the mop, and bucket, and working around Mr. Lobster was involuntary. The lobster watched Cade, and Cade got the floor as dry as he could, for as long as he could, and he placed the *Caution: Wet floor!* sign where it was visible to all shoppers.

The children loved to scoot across the wet floor and make faces at the old lobster. His shell was dark black and stood out against the muddy brown canvas of water. The children grabbed their lips and pulled their faces into ghoulish looks—tongues sticking out. Cade encouraged it. Told the kids that Mr. Lobster loved the attention. The kids did this every day, as long as their parents would allow.

***

It was five o'clock when he looked up from stocking the peanut butter jars. Cade tore his apron off and ran to the back to place it on a hook. He left the box cutter inside, and he placed his nametag there, too. On his way out the swinging door, he saw Florence from Human Resources talking with Bill Clip in the manager's office. Cade didn't want to eavesdrop, but he could tell it was heated. He paused long enough to catch, "It's getting too serious."

"I'm fine. I can run this store in my sleep," Clip said, coughing and blowing his nose into a handkerchief.

"That's not the point. Your work is affecting the *customers*," she said. "One today came to the customer service desk and said, 'He sneezed on my rib-eye steaks. He didn't mean to, but he did.' What do you say to that? Do you remember doing that?"

"It was an accident. Won't happen again," he muttered.

"I can give you some time off, but I don't know if it'll help," she said. "Do you? Your doctor said it was chronic. What was it . . . allergic rhinitis? Is that right?" her voice rose, as she said it.

Clip cleared his throat, as a form of answering.

"I'm going to have to give you some leave. Who could you train to do your job while you're out six weeks tops? If it's any longer, I'm going to have to hire someone else, and Bigsby will move on without you," she said.

Silence followed, then Cade could hear Clip just above a hoarse whisper, "I know who, but I don't like it," and the door closed shut.

Cade backed out of the space and walked to the front of the store. Passing Aisle 1 on the way, he thought of Mercedes and picked up all nine bottles of carrot juice that would go bad tomorrow. He wasn't sure why he did it, but he knew it was the right thing to do. She would be proud of him. He couldn't share it with her, because she was already in Lexington, attending her equine program. Cade missed her like crazy, and it'd only been two weeks since graduation. Two weeks!

Cade put the bottles into a plastic bag, then re-bagged it for extra support. He walked out the automatic sliding doors, past the Citronella bamboo torches, and into the humid Kentucky heat. It would be great to be fishing at Cumberland, Cade thought, and realized he hadn't said that since Spoonbill. The thought of a strong lake breeze rushing past his face felt almost real. He hopped into the old Ford pickup, Abbott's ride, and drove back across town, past Cobank Mountain, and crunched gravel up to his home. He decided he'd share his bottles of carrot juice with Abbott and Mom. He'd freeze the others for later.

He recalled Bill Clip's comment about needing to take time off, and his argument with Florence in HR. His illness sounded like something from a sci-fi movie M might've recommended.

He waved as he entered the hallway and gave the drinks to his mom and next-door neighbor.

# CHAPTER TWELVE

Cade picked his apron up and instinctively went to Mr. Lobster.

The leak was worse. The heavy-duty epoxy glue was no longer masking the degradation. Water spouted in a constant leak from the back of the tank. His stomach hurt from all of the carrot juice he drank the night before.

"Faster," Bill groaned, behind his handkerchief. "And when you're finished meet me in *my* office."

Cade mock-saluted, and kept mopping the floor, knowing it was no use. The leak was there to stay. He squeegeed the floor as best he could, and let the dripping continue, as he trudged to the back office. He inhaled deeply and crossed the small man's threshold. The dimly lit room felt cavernous to him, despite its confined space.

"Over here," Bill Clip gestured to a swivel-backed chair. "Sit down. Florence will be here in a second."

"What's all this about?" Cade knowingly asked.

"You'll learn soon enough."

Florence walked in and perched on a stack of manila folders piled high. "This won't take but a second, Mr. Rainy," she said. He appreciated her lack of condescension. "We have every bit of faith in you to be the best *replacement* for Bill, on a *temporary* basis, of course." She smiled, looking in Clip's direction.

Cade saw that his boss' smile was less hopeful than Florence's.

"What's wrong with hi—" Cade started.

"Never mind. That's HR business," Clip interrupted. "Florence and I have it under control. I just need to step out for a few weeks is all," he said, shifting uncomfortably in his chair.

"Maybe more," she countered. "But we have every prayer in Bethel Baptist and other Seton churches going up to God right now. You should pray, too. We want to see Mr. Clip back on his feet."

Cade felt his head bob in agreement. "Right? But, you want me to be the manager? While he's out?" he asked, trying to fake-believe it.

"So, we're in agreement that you start straight away? You know what Bill does day-to-day as manager, correct?" Florence pried.

"He doesn't know *everything,*" Clip argued. "But . . . most of it I've shown him."

"Fine. But, the HR paperwork starts today. Get your things and get better," she demanded, turning to leave the room.

"Florence?" Clip said as she exited. She paused, turned. "When do I go on leave exactly?" he asked, fidgeting with the manila folders she'd almost knocked over when she stood.

"Tomorrow. Be sure you're out of here and away from Bigsby. Okay? We don't want any more health violations."

Clip waved her off and turned to Cade. He wiped his nose with a tattered napkin he retrieved from his pocket. "Listen to me," he said, eyes bloodshot, worse than the day before. "As I get *better,* I want this space taken care of like a newborn. Got it? Clean as a whistle."

Cade looked at the sickly man. Being manager would be a great responsibility, but not like this. Not forced. He didn't want that. He looked to the door but Florence was already gone.

"Rainy, did you hear? You start tomorrow. So get out of here. I'm manager for one more day at least. You take the day and go try to find something close to a manager's backbone. And tomorrow, the store is yours . . ."

"What about training. I thought—"

"You've watched me plenty. You've seen my binder. Do as I do, and you'll not make too big a mess, I hope." He wheezed. "Now go." He coughed, pointing at the door, unable to cover his mouth in time.

Cade back-tracked out of the office and kept his head down all the way to the lobster tank. The leak was gushing worse. He saw the water level below the lobster's eyes. Mr. Lobster looked confused and startled by the chaos. The brown water was disappearing, and his dark exoskeleton was now exposed to a suffocating plastic box. Cade knew there wasn't much time for him left. On instinct, he scooted the mop bucket out of the way, and plunged his arms down into the tank. The lobster struck at him, but he was too confused and disoriented to clamp down onto Cade's hand. He missed and clamped empty, brown water. Cade grabbed him by his large tail and pulled him from the tank. Clutching him and running for the front of the store, Cade didn't pause for Florence's reaction. He burst out the front entrance, dodging a confused shopper, and hopped into the Ford. Cade found it difficult to drive and keep the old lobster from committing suicide on their trip home.

***

Hollie Rainy was mortified at Mr. Lobster's predicament. She didn't offer to take and cook him. "He's that old one they've had in the tank forever," she exclaimed. "That thing is like a fixture at Bigsby," she said. "I've spoken to it when I shopped many a time."

Abbott Mize stood in the kitchen, sipping a cup of black coffee. "Looks good for the pot," was all he offered, retrieving a metal one from under the Rainy's sink. In a matter of seconds, Abbott had butter, herbs, and lemon juice from Hollie's fridge. He poured about four quarts of water into the pot and set it to a boil. He said, "Put the old man in there, and we'll have dinner in no time."

Cade trusted his mom with most things, but he had learned over time, as neighbors, that Abbott was an expert on a multitude of others beyond their family norm. Much like teaching Mercedes to break horses, including Clay, and being a genuine reason for why she was in Lexington now, Abbott taught Cade to trust him. He was Mom's boyfriend now, and in a way, they were Abbott's new family since losing his own to country music fame. He became a mentor of sorts. Cade looked down at Mr. Lobster and saw the weakening eyes, his dissipating strength. Instead of remorse for taking him out of the saltwater tank and driving him across town, he felt disgust. This critter caused him so much pain over the months. Would he have even needed the mop if this crustacean had died a while back? Cade reached out to Abbott and handed off the crustacean—Mr. Lobster, his pinchers slicing the air—as he looked for one final skirmish.

The water bubbled in the metal pot, sending some over the brim and down into the stove coils causing a loud hissing sound and lots of steam. "Turn it down a bit!" Abbott urged.

The squirming lobster looked for an exit, and finding none, suddenly stopped wrestling, stopped pinching entirely. It looked like complete resignation, Cade thought. Mr. Lobster went down into the hissing sounds of the pot, and Abbott said, "Lid. Lid, pronto!"

Hollie found one and Abbott plopped it down on top. What happened next surprised Cade even more. He'd always been told by teachers that lobsters screamed (and screeched) while being boiled alive, but Mr. Lobster did not. As if resigned to the afterlife, he didn't make a peep. He couldn't be heard over the hissing water, and Abbott said more than once, "He's taking it well."

"How does one take boiling alive well?" Hollie asked.

"Without clawing for the exits," Abbott said. "A dignified death."

No one spoke while the timer counted down on the stove. When the time was up, Cade walked over and peered into the pot. It was amazing! Mr. Lobster wasn't fighting anymore, and he was a bright, intense, rich red color. The boiling water turned his shell a new hue. Cade couldn't think of the right description, but he was beautiful. And Cade saw that he didn't look like he was in pain anymore. He clapped his hands together, and Hollie turned to him.

"I know you and *it* were close, but—" she said, gesturing to the pot.

"Maybe he's in a better place," Cade admitted.

"I'm going to move him to this platter and get the accoutrements ready. Everyone wash their hands?" Abbott said in his strong Kentucky accent.

Cade smiled. "I'm not going to eat him. You and Mom go ahead," he said, starting to walk away.

Abbott caught his forearm in a light grip. "This is unlike anything you've ever had, young man. I promise."

Cade looked at Mr. Lobster on the platter. "I bet he's tough and sour. As much of his own filth he's had down there in the tank. I bet he—"

"Just get a plate," Hollie scolded.

Cade did as she said, and he brought his plate to the platter. Abbott broke off a big claw and *whacked* it with a small hammer from the Rainys' closet. "Here, take this claw and get the meat from it. Don't let any go to waste," he said.

Cade extracted the meat, and it was a lot. It was Mr. Lobster's bigger claw, one Cade had thought of only as a weapon. Now, he pulled the meat out, and the smell was intoxicating.

Abbott pushed the melted butter over to him and Hollie. "Dig in," he smiled. "Tell me that tastes just like chicken and I'll smack both of you sideways."

Cade let Hollie go first, and she dipped the lobster claw gingerly into the butter. "Here's to Mr. Lobster," she joked and put the wet claw meat into her mouth, as her smile held its place. She made an *mmm* sound.

Cade dipped the claw into the butter slowly like she had and brought the aroma to his nose, before hesitantly putting the lobster into his mouth. The butter and meat fell into immediate favor with his taste buds. *It was sweet and rich and delicious. Mr. Lobster was worth it!* And before he knew it, Hollie and he were dipping again and again into the butter sauce—devouring the claw meat.

"Save some for me!" Abbott kidded, busting the other claw and generously slathering the meat into the butter and bringing the fork to his lips. "Mr. Lobster grew better with age," he said, swallowing the crustacean with vigor.

Cade agreed. Mr. Lobster had aged well. He'd always heard that the older an animal became—the less tasty. But, this wasn't so with the lobster. The three ate all of the claw meat and surrounding area down to the shell. When they came to the tail, Abbott paused.

"If you two knuckleheads thought *that* was good," he said, pointing to their graveyard of work. "Then, you're about to see what all the rage for lobsters is about and why they cost an arm and a leg. Why do you think no one ever bought Mr. Lobster?" he asked, stalling.

Cade knew and felt guilty all of a sudden. "The price tag," he said. "Too much for Seton's budget."

Abbott agreed, and held the tail in the air and said, "And people just saw him in town and thought he was a big ole crawfish. A mud bug. But he's not. This is what makes him the top of the menu at fancy restaurants." Abbott removed the shell from the tail and set it onto the platter.

Cade inspected it. "Looks like a brain from my old biology class."

"Don't think too much about it. Just take the butter. Cut this portion here and here, and we'll third it," Abbott said.

Hollie was licking her lips and stopped when Cade saw her. He lifted her a third of the tail with his fork and knife and did the same for Abbott. Then, they dipped all three portions into the butter and ate in unison. A chorus of agreement rose from the table, and it was the first time Cade ever thought he'd heard such sounds. It wasn't his mom's lack of cooking ability either. It was the quality of the lobster. The rich, sweet meat and the salty hints of the butter and the zest from the lemon juice and herb flakes made it succulent. Cade ate without looking up, and when the colossal meal was gone, he felt happy with the day, except for his theft.

Cade pushed himself away from the table, said, "They let me go early today. Tomorrow I'm . . ."

Abbott and Hollie looked at him, waited on him to finish. The large shell remnants rested on the platter between them, their triangle of happiness.

Cade burped. "And tomorrow I'm supposed to be manager at Bigsby," he said. "Bill Clip has some sort of ailment," he added. "Sick as a dog."

Neither moved, and then Hollie stood up, came around the table, and hugged him. She said, "You're going to be the best! I knew Mr. Clip was ill, but I didn't know he was letting you take over."

"Congrats to you, Cade!" Abbott said. Then, after a pause, "Haven would be proud."

The words held all three in the room, as the strong seafood aroma made Cade light-headed. Hollie said, "I better get this cleaned up. We don't want to stare at it too long. Otherwise, we might start expecting this every meal. And we can't have that, can we?"

Abbott said, "Cade. You did the right thing coming back home. In fact, I want to show you something else. Teach you something. What do you say?"

"I'm not really feeling like a lesson, *Mr. Mize*," Cade said, aware of the annoyance it caused.

Abbott cringed, but his smile didn't disappear. He pointed to his now-all-white hair. "I guess I'm deserving that title more and more these days, ain't I?"

Cade didn't answer; he watched Hollie put the shells into a separate plastic trash bag and tie it up to mask the smell. He just wanted his mom to be happy. Abbott was a great guy, too. His presence at mealtime made the evenings more enjoyable.

"Won't take no time at all. I think you'll pick it up right quick. Being a fast learner like yourself and all," he tried to joke. "I mean, they don't let just anyone move into management without one iota of training," he continued.

"It won't take long?"

"Have you back before sundown," Abbott promised.

"We're not moving rocks or building fences, are we?" Cade asked, looking out the door.

"Not today," Abbott said, exhaling and hitching his tight waistband up a little higher, above his rounded belly.

Cade followed the man out to the Ford, and the two waved to his mom as they backed out the driveway.

***

The truck maneuvered across Cobank Mountain, down its steep roads and in a direction Cade hadn't traveled in years: Cumberland Lake.

The brakes squeaked, and Abbott pulled the truck into a parking spot just a few feet from the water's edge.

"What're we doing out here?" Cade's voice asked, shrill like it had been in middle school.

"I wanted to teach you out *here*," Abbott said, blank-faced and staring at the water. Boats flew by over the white-capped waves. "It requires water, as you can see."

When the words left Abbott, they mingled with the zooms and zings of the personal watercrafts passing his visage. Had he heard the old man straight?

"Water. How much water?" Cade asked, getting defensive.

"I want to teach you to swim again," Abbott said, without hesitation.

Cade looked him over—good and thorough—and didn't see a chink in the man's armor. "I'm almost eighteen," Cade said. "What makes you think I can't teach myself?"

"I've heard you say you wish you could re-learn more than once," Abbott said, chomping on his loose leaf tobacco.

"And you're the man for the job?" Cade pressured, growing nervous.

"I'm willing to teach until the sun goes down. But after that, well, I leave when I can't see those water moccasins." He smiled.

The way he just threw out worst-case scenarios always baffled Cade. He admitted it did help with the nerves, but it was all so matter-of-fact. It made Cade wonder how he was always so turned off to what scared others to death. Batting away these thoughts, Cade said, "'Til sundown? Then, we get the heck out of here?" He looked up the hill and away from Cumberland, away from anything resembling Spoonbill Dam.

"My word," Abbott said, crossing his heart. "Was I wrong about the lobster?"

Cade didn't answer but knew Abbott was rarely wrong. He figured if he was going to learn to conquer this fear, to be an *Explorer* like his dad, he had to take the first step with someone again. Abbott Mize was as capable a teacher as any.

He gestured toward the water, and Abbott led the way to the swaying dock.

***

The lake was a ruckus, and the dock swayed to and fro. Pontoon boats churned up the water, and the sun's reflection made it difficult to stare at the water beneath them. Bass boats skittered up and down the shoreline of the Cumberland and a few boaters waved at Abbott.

"Do you know *everyone* in Seton?" Cade asked, trying his best to steady himself on the dock's rocking frame, not looking up.

"Treat it like you're surfing. Or, like you imagine surfing to be," Abbott explained. "Don't fight the wake from the boats, but let the motion guide you back and forth. This dock is fastened to the mainland. You are right *here*, and I won't let you die." He smiled.

"Another joke? Really?" Cade asked.

Abbott waved to some people fishing on the adjacent bank from where they stood. "Move over here so this boat can get loaded onto their trailer coming down the hill."

The two waited for a Ranger fishing boat to be fastened and secured to its trailer, and a forest green Dodge Ram pulled it up the rocky incline.

"Now, as I was saying. You can't resist the motion in this small ocean." Mize laughed. "If you let the water move you, you'll be just fine. On top of the water that is . . ." he added.

"Huh?" Cade asked.

"On top of the water, it's okay to go with the rocking motion. But, once we're swimming, you'll have to resist the water's flowing currents. Swimming is an action. It takes work."

Cade stared at him blankly.

"You have to do something. Getting tossed about doesn't work so well when you're down in the water. You have to fight to keep your head above it. Now, I don't mean beat the water to death or anything."

"I know," Cade said, arms crossed, keeping himself from shaking with fear.

"You have to do it like this." And without another word, Abbott Mize stripped down to his skivvies and jumped into the choppy waves and resurfaced about fifty yards from the dock—instantly swimming back in a blaze.

Cade watched and saw him cutting the water like sharks he'd seen on TV do. Abbott moved with precision, and he hardly looked his age in the deep, dark waters. He went arm-over-head and breathed in between each movement. He did it without goggles or gear. Cade looked on from the dock and moved out of the way of a Jet Ski being loaded.

"That's a fast old man," the Jet Ski owner said, stepping past Cade. "You and him racing?"

Cade just shook his head and stared at the movement. Abbott's upper body was rocketing and his legs were kicking up very little water. He looked like a torpedo, and it didn't seem possible.

"How did you?" Cade asked, when Abbott resurfaced at the dock's edge barely winded.

"Normally I would keep my secrets to myself, but I'm in the giving spirit this evening," he said. "Did you see my motion?"

Cade told him about the movement of the arms, the limited splashing, and very little kicking he saw.

"Good. This shouldn't take no time. A bright student like yourself. It's important to propel yourself forward and slice through the water in as direct a route as you can," he said. "Give it a go, and I'll be right here."

"Give it a go? Just jump in? What if I sink?"

"It's not a matter of if, but when," Abbott encouraged. "I suggest you get in and go ahead and get the first worry over with. Besides, I'm quicker than anything else out here . . . well, almost."

Cade's mind started to race, but before he could worry anymore, he heard Abbott say, "If you don't get in, I'm going to pull you."

Fear took over. The thought of being dragged into the abyss without his consent was the worst fear imaginable. He dove in awkwardly in his boxers and belly flopped on the uneven, stronger-than-it-looked surface.

Instantly, his stomach hurt, and Cade knew a welt would form on his abdomen. As he clawed to the surface, it felt like ankle weights were attached to him. He started to struggle and thrash the molecules back and forth. This wasn't like wading for trout at all.

To his surprise, he felt hands reach up under his armpits and pry him to the surface. Rather than fight it, he relaxed, and he was gasping for air in a few seconds.

"Easy does it," Abbott's gruff voice soothed. "No need to drink more than your share. It'll be here all summer. Or, at least I hope you leave the rest of us some."

Cade fought him off, and Abbott graciously dropped him back into his nightmare. "Abbott!" he gurgled between swallowing more mouthfuls of the lake. "I'm going to kill yyouu." And again he went under the surface and down, down, down he sank.

The strong hands gripped him, and he felt them patiently drag him into the air, and into the blue sky above. Again, he gasped. "Give me a chance to figure it out!"

A pontoon boat loaded with six or seven family members chugged past them and waved to Abbott. He returned the gesture but Cade seized up when the hand left him. He knew it looked funny; him being almost a grown man and coddled this way.

"Dad said he was going to teach me how to do this better," he said, still coughing from the muddy water.

"He's here all right. I know he wouldn't miss this for the world," Abbott said.

"What's that mean?"

"Just what I said. You need to do more paddling and less talking, if we're going to figure this out before dark," Abbott confided.

The word *dark* had a sobering effect on Cade's attitude. He glanced up at the sky, and even though there were hours between then and bedtime, he said, "Tell me what I need to do, and I'll do it. Whatever."

Abbott said, "I'm going to do one more lap, and I want you to follow alongside me. Don't take your eyes off of me. If you do, I know you'll fare like Simon Peter's brief walk on water. But, if you watch . . . and swim like I am, and don't think so much on sinking you'll learn a funny thing. You start *doing* more than *doubting*. Got me?"

Abbott's question required no answer. He let go of Cade's underarms, and in one fluid motion, stretched out and began his freestyle swim again—only going at about a third of the speed he'd used the first time, making sure Cade stayed parallel to him.

Cade's mind couldn't think about drowning because Abbott was just crazy enough to leave him. He stretched out and mimicked the older man's style; he freestyled and let his arms do the churning through the water. Breathing was his only real obstacle between strokes, but Cade learned that if they were perfectly in sync, he could breathe and swim in the exact same rhythm as Abbott.

He did this, and he no longer imagined the heaviness of his body—out in the middle of the lake, turning toward shore, and the long swim back to the dock. The only distraction was the humming sound he heard in the water. Later, Abbott told him it was boat propellers making such a chatter. He was curious about how the fish dealt with the sound. If he was a fish, he admitted, it might drive him crazy. But Cade had a larger concern when he arrived at the dock.

"Let's go off to the side and float," Abbott said. "It's a lot harder to stay in place in water," he added. "You'll find that just keeping yourself afloat and treading water is one of the hardest tasks."

Cade focused on the movement of Abbott's body, the way he never seemed to panic but would paddle in just the right moments like a frog. He mimicked this and kept his head above water for several minutes. *Can I do this without him?* The boat noises reappeared, and he noticed his neck going below the surface. Slowly and surely he was sinking again. He felt the hands under his arms.

"Don't let the fear make you lose focus of this one thing: *survival,*" Abbott offered.

The notion of survival brought back Cade's fixation with Dad and this lake. He fought the distraction of the boat propellers and the wake sloshing against his neck, this dock. He said, "I'm picturing a dog paddling. It looks like this," he laughed.

"Whatever it takes to keep you afloat," the old man said.

The two swam for another thirty minutes, until Cade said his legs were feeling heavy. Abbott made a point to get him out of the water, before the lesson was lost to swimmer's cramp. They climbed the hill to the pickup and toweled off.

"Got something to say?" Abbott asked.

Cade was unsure of his meaning but felt the excitement brimming within him. All he could think to say was, "It was all right," with a shrug of his shoulders. He tried to play it cool, but Abbott patted him on the back.

"What?" Cade asked.

Abbott said, "You weren't too bad out there."

Cade said, "Good teacher, I guess."

A two-story houseboat went by the dock, and he imagined what it would be like to live on Cumberland, a lake he hadn't seen, let alone swam in, for years. Now, he saw this massive boat and wondered how it floated. He knew it had buoys and propulsion that kept it from going under. Didn't he have the same thing? Maybe the difference was between a mind and a motor, he thought. The boat had a motor and a mind behind the motor. His body had a motor and a mind behind it, too. Didn't it?

He looked across the truck's cab and saw Abbott staring at him. "What?"

"How do you disappear like that?" Abbott asked.

"My mind's like your swimming skills," Cade retorted. "Quick and dangerous."

The two laughed.

"Anybody that dines on lobster and learns to swim in two-hundred-feet-deep water all before bedtime should be commended," Abbott beamed, starting the truck.

Cade was content in knowing the lake's depth. *200 feet!* He still felt the pat on his back. And, he knew, Dad was proud of him somewhere.

# CHAPTER THIRTEEN

His confidence soared after the lake swim. Cade marched into the Bigsby Food Market the next day and started with his managerial duties. Bill Clip left detailed notes in his binder. Cade cleaned the leaky spots around the tank, disassembling it quickly. Before what little traffic came through the market before lunch, he discussed hours, paychecks, and timesheets with Florence. She proved most helpful, and even offered to point him to the most up-to-date roster of people assigned to work through that weekend.

Before he knew it, confidence was exuding from his pores. Cade waved to customers and tried to be more helpful with matters he remembered Clip ordering people to do. His co-workers smiled, and several gave him pats on the back. Stock boy, Terry Wilson, said, "Way to go, boss!"

Cade took it to heart and felt like his promotion was his entrance into the *real* workforce. But, something still didn't resonate as completely as he hoped it would.

It was early summer, and the meat department was booming. People were demanding sirloin steaks and pork loins for barbequing. Cade didn't have time to pause running from the front to the back of the market—even for lunch. He especially lost his momentum at three o'clock, when he learned that his second shift butcher, Paulie, was missing in action. Did Clip just cover for absent workers? Cade couldn't remember, but it didn't seem like him.

Picking up the back office phone and scanning the office rolodex, he found Saul's number and dialed him. He was off today; his only other meat department worker. The phone rang and rang. No answer.

Cade set the phone receiver down into its cradle and admitted defeat. It was his first of the day, and without Paulie, the second shift would take him to his knees. It required not only working to cover the cutting, but also restocking the display cases, and cleaning (and disinfecting) all of the butcher machines by closing time. With two people it was tough to do it all by 10:00 p.m. already, and by himself, and no help leading into the dinner rush, he knew ten would become eleven-thirty, easy. Yet, he put his head down and worked as hard as he could—not focusing on the clock.

***

Family after family came into and out of the Bigsby Food Market requesting meat trays and special cuts. There was even a surge of sockeye salmon filet requests at one point, and Cade found himself traying fish, offering samples of rotisserie chicken breasts, and trying to re-shelve the depleted filet mignons. All to no avail, he felt. What brought the progress to a crashing halt was a customer who came through not two hours after Paulie no-showed, working the perimeter of the store. The man walked absentmindedly around the produce and dairy sections and bypassed Aisle 1 and eventually arrived back at the meat counter. The scraggly-faced creep peered into the display case and poked his dirty fingernails into the filet mignons and started rearranging them. Then, he picked up one, two, and eventually, six packages and shoved them all into his handheld Bigsby grocery basket—leaving only one steak behind.

Cade's busy schedule only permitted him to see the depleted row when he looked up from slicing a large roast beef for Mercer's wife, Millie. She thanked him, said the thickness was just right for lunch sandwiches, and left.

When he did lift his head up from the deli slicer, he saw the devastation and instinctively went to the video footage. This was a trick Clip had shown him over the months he'd watched him. So, Cade looked at the four cameras and saw the criminal re-emerge at Aisle 14, holding a bag of Cheetos. M would have something to say, if she were here, he thought.

Sure enough, Cade saw his long-nailed hands drop the Cheetos into the grocery basket; the spot where the filet had rested just moments ago was now empty. And, the man walked with an awkward shuffle. Cade tapped the screen, "Gotcha buddy!" He hustled to the store's main section and let the managerial doors shut behind him.

When he rounded the corner, he saw the man look up and make eye contact. Rather than duck his head and run, he kept the shuffle motion up, moving ever so slightly to the opposite end. Cade could see the man's mind spinning, thinking: *Break for it!* When he scooted around the opposite end, closest to the store's entrance, the criminal dodged Martin, offering free cheese samples, and almost made it to the door. But, Cade's youth won out. He blockaded the door with his frame, and to avoid a nasty collision in the Citronella display area, he asked, winded, "May I ask if you found everything all right today, sir?"

Cade's voice laying it on thick didn't deter the criminal in the slightest, he saw, because the man wheezed, "Everything was right where I thought it would be. Thank ya. Now if you'll kindly step aside. My kid is waiting on me in the car." He grinned through crooked teeth, playing dumb better than anyone Cade knew.

"Fine," Cade said, hands raised in a bargaining look. "I didn't want to have to do this, but you leave me no choice. To avoid the law, I'm going to have to ask you point blank: did you steal the steaks?"

The dirty fingernails play-drummed on his pant legs, and the man didn't make eye contact. "My kid's in the car," he said again, more conviction in his raspy voice this time. "She's hungry," he pleaded, his eyes lifting to Cade's, head still downcast. "C'mon. Would ya let someone in *your* family go hungry?"

The shift in questioning caught Cade off-guard. "Excuse me? Did you take them? If so, just spill. I'm too busy to get the cops over here." He exhaled. "Understand?"

The dirty, poorly manicured man lifted up both pant legs and the trays of meat fell onto the ground. His gaze returned to the floor. "Are we through here?" he asked through clenched teeth.

"You did the right thing," Cade offered.

"Try telling that to my girl's empty belly," he said, not waiting for a reply, as he trudged through the store's exit, away from the video cameras.

Cade picked up the steaks and returned them to the meat department—only able to celebrate the tiny victory alone. He glanced at each tray and realized the twin packs averaged almost thirty bucks apiece. "180 bucks!" he bragged to no one. But the moment was short-lived as the bell rang, and a family needing a party-sized order of half-inch thick boneless pork loins took their time in selecting the perfect pig. Cade took it into the closed space of the department, cut the pork loin as best he could. Meat wasn't his specialty at the Bigsby, and he was learning quickly that he just wanted to survive.

No sooner than he was able to get the pork loin Styrofoam-trayed on the pork table (because the pork, beef, and fish were separated to avoid cross-contamination), the bell rang again. Cade took the plastic wrap and sealed the pork loin and offered it to the family.

The newest shopper asked if he had any Tyson boneless chicken thighs in the back. "All of the packs out here are gone." The old man frowned. "My family loves those fried better than anything. Can you help?"

Cade, never able to refuse a kind request, went into the back freezer and climbed the metal racks searching for the Tyson chicken boxes. When he found one labeled *chicken thighs,* he noted it was all the way at the top. *How do I get this down?* He found a full-size ladder and angled the heavy box onto it and let gravity saunter it to the ground. Then, he pried the box open and brought out three containers and the man bought all three. "Many thanks," he beamed.

***

Cade didn't want to see the clock but admitted his last bits of energy were dwindling. The store felt empty without Clip constantly maneuvering around him and the others. Suddenly he thought: What others? He'd seen Florence just briefly, when he'd entered the store, and Martin offering cheese samples during the robbery attempt. And there was the stock boy, Terry Wilson. Apart from these, he couldn't remember anyone else. Three people on such a busy day! *How will I make it the rest of summer with staff flaking out like Paulie?* He might've known Clip was out and wanted to give it to me, Cade reasoned.

Then, a miracle happened: Paulie moseyed into the meat department with his apron on, and he picked up the chicken breast box instinctively, put it on a metal cart, and wheeled it out for stocking the case like nothing was wrong. When he returned, rather than scold him, Cade simply patted him on the back, "Glad you're here, Paulie. You have no idea!"

Paulie looked a little on the fritz: shaggy hair, glazed over eyes.

"You gonna stay until close?"

"Yeah. Sorry about that. I totally slept in, and my folks woke me up and said, "Paulie, don't you have work?" I was like whoa, yeah, you're right. And then, I scooted down here to Bigsby as quick as I could."

Too relieved to be angry and too hungry to say much more, Cade muttered, "Glad you made it," and said, "I'm gonna grab a bite. Then, I'll help as much as I can, while I see the others and check on them, too."

"That's right. You got promoted. Congrats, boss man," Paulie said, gazing off in the direction of the absent Mr. Lobster. "Whoa. What happened to our *pet*?"

"He finally went home," Cade answered, pleased with himself—the end of the proverbial mess. The taste of the sweet meat was still prevalent in his nose and mouth; the recent memory made his mouth water.

Turning to the rotisserie ovens, Cade saw a whole chicken that was fully cooked, oven alarm beeping. He said, "I'm going to demo this chicken to customers," and left it at that. When he had the bird spliced down to small sampling cups, he took a few for himself and went to the break room to analyze the notes Clip left.

***

His hands shook from the constant pace he'd maintained. Cade tried to grip an ink pen and write down the numbers of whole chickens skewered, racks of ribs cooked, and salmon fillets demoed throughout, but he couldn't put pen to paper. The shaking became worse, and the logbook seemed to taunt him. How did Clip do it? Then, he remembered: Bill Clip hadn't been able to. He remembered the illness he'd overheard Florence discussing. Now, Clip was at home on leave. The omen wasn't good, Cade thought.

When he finally did get the chicken into his stomach with some Yoo Hoo chasing it down, he licked his lips and popped his knuckles. Cade glanced at the clock to see how quickly the day was moving. To his amazement, it was already past eight o'clock. The store was set to close at ten, but even with clean-up initiated by eight-thirty, it would still be ten-thirty at the earliest. The thought sobered him. *What happens when we're all that's here . . . three days in a row? How do I take a day off?* Suddenly, the walls felt as if they were closing in like they did in that Star Wars movie. The suffocation felt real.

He entered the meat department, "Paulie, initiate clean-up procedures."

"But, man, there're like four families all making demands out there right now. How do I work around them?" his eyes wide, distant.

"Let me take care of the customers. I'll help as best I can, when I'm not up front. Just focus on breaking the saw machine down, sanitizing everything as best you can, and squeegeeing. Got it?"

"Right on," he said, putting his efforts into getting the soap and water buckets ready.

True to his word, Cade got the four orders of pork loin, rib eye, short ribs, and ahi tuna filet out to customers and went to the front of the Bigsby. The clock read nine-fifteen at the store's entrance. He flagged a sweaty, salt-and-pepper-haired Florence down. "How goes it?" he asked.

"Making it. You doing okay? First day and all?"

"I've seen it all so many times before, but doing it all at once is harder than it looks."

She paused, and he imagined her waiting for something else. Maybe a phrase like "And that's why I can't do this" or, "Clip was wrong to recommend me." But he didn't relent in his quest to make it to closing time.

"I'll get the cash drawers cleaned and counted down and make sure there aren't any overages or losses. If you can close customer service and returns down, I'd appreciate it," he caught himself saying.

"I've done this longer than you've been shaving."

Florence was kind to an extent, but he'd crossed it with this comment. He waited for more snarky words, but none came.

"Got it. Well, I'm going to keep helping Martin, Terry, and Paulie break down the back sections. Paulie is already getting things sanitized. We might be out by ten-thirty," he said, sounding as hopeful as he could.

Then, she folded her arms. "Doesn't matter to me whether you're out at ten-thirty or not. I go home at ten regardless."

He didn't take the bait. "I thought two people . . . er, management had to close the store together? Is that not true?"

"HR makes a lot of the rules, and I say, working two shifts is as far as I go. Nothing can keep me here another thirty minutes, because *someone* didn't come in when he was supposed to." She pointed back to Paulie's area.

It was a catch-22, but Cade knew the right thing to do was to stand by Paulie and see the cleaning through. He was more tired than he ever remembered.

He told Florence he'd see her the next day and bid her a good night. Then, he spun on his heels and helped Martin get the remaining cheese samples put away—eating a few and laughing a bit, before he told Martin to come back tomorrow. Cade went down the canned aisles and found Terry.

"Great first day, huh boss?" the boy exclaimed. "Busy enough for you?"

"For two of me and maybe a third," Cade answered. "Listen, I appreciate your enthusiasm, and I wanted to say have a great night. We'll see you tomorrow," and with Terry's last can of green beans placed on the shelf, facing outward for future customers—he, too, left the Bigsby, the front clock reading ten.

Finally, Cade went to check on Paulie and saw the teen fidgeting with the meat department's blood drain. "You okay down there?" he asked, in the direction of the clog Paulie was trying to remove.

"As good as I can be, boss man. These chunks get stuck in here, and there's no one to get 'em out. Ya know? It's not good for the pipes."

Cade looked at the backflow of bloody water and soap suds. "You hitting all of those metal holders with sanitizing spray, after it's washed thoroughly?"

"You know it," Paulie agreed. "If it was cleaner it'd be on display in the CDC," he laughed.

Cade joined in and worked with the radio dial. He found some old Motown hits and let the tunes drift through the fluorescent-lighted space. Cade scrubbed and broke down; Paulie sanitized once the clog was removed. Finally, both took turns squeegeeing, and Cade hit the lights off, leaving everything to drip dry.

He walked Paulie to the time card station and both punched their tickets. "See you tomorrow, hombre," Paulie said, disappearing down the lonely Seton highway on his skateboard.

Cade got into Abbott's Ford, the last in the lot, and cranked the engine to life. This was just one day. *What happens when it's a string of busy months? Busy years? How did Clip deal?*

*Simple. He didn't.* The truck climbed the hills and maneuvered Cobank Mountain like a dream, and by the time his head hit the pillow that's exactly what he did all night.

# CHAPTER FOURTEEN

Cade was sore from head to toe, as he rolled out of bed. At the sound of his alarm, he looked to see he'd overslept. Cade admitted work wasn't satisfactory in the least. It *did* keep his mind off M, her bronze-colored skin. The perfume-scented letters in his mailbox kept him in a constant state of distraction. She'd wanted to write letters by hand, because email was too easy and didn't leave anything tangible, she said. Now, it was mid-June and there didn't look to be any release this summer.

At the store's entrance, he unlocked the automatic sliding doors and turned on the electronic switch that made them rock closed and open. Cade stepped inside and noticed how dingy the store's perimeter—walls, rain-stained ceiling, and grimy tiles—made the establishment seem. It wasn't a welcoming place, even though the grime looked completely standard.

Florence exhaled. "Good morning to you, Mr. Rainy," as if she'd said it the past fifteen years. The familiarity of it unnerved him. Cade looked to the exit and considered a quick getaway. *I could go home and Explore.* But, even that activity, exploring the cave he'd mapped so well, now seemed dull and ancient without his friends. "Mornin'," he muttered in response.

The predictability of what Florence would say next was unsettling, because he'd heard her say it countless times to a distracted, determined Bill Clip. Sure enough, her mouth opened and out came, "If today's like yesterday, we're in for a doozy." Coughing into her closed fist like a war vet. Her face was always poker game ready. Cade turned his back to her.

Now she was saying these same things to him, as if he were Clip. He didn't want it. "Listen, Florence—"

"Flo is fine, honey. I've known your momma since we were grade school girls," she said. "It's okay if you want to smoke in the manager's office, too. I do all the time."

And she did. Cade knew the musty smell well, and it sickened him every time he entered the back office. He shook his head curtly. "I'm fine. Smoking isn't something I've developed a taste for yet."

She shrugged her shoulders and walked that direction. "Suit yourself. Give me twenty, and I'll be up at the customer service desk to save the world from certain destruction."

Florence was HR of the Bigsby Food Market, but also customer service manager (and loss prevention specialist). She was a *three-in-one employee,* Cade remembered overhearing Bill Clip say before his departure. He'd said it was *The Bigsby Way,* as if this explanation explained all the concern people had for someone working three jobs on any given day.

Cade felt her pain just in his first day at the management helm, and the summer heat would bring most of Seton into the store, out of the Appalachian hills. They'd be seeking ice chests, Igloo coolers, ice bag after ice bag, and a never-ending demand for ripe, seedless watermelons. Cade didn't know when watermelons first lost their seeds, or, people started requesting them that way, but he figured it was a result of genetic manipulation. Now, Bigsby only carried the seedless kind. Moms with long, gaggling lines of children in tow would enter the grocery, saying, "Don't touch the melons. It's my job."

Sure enough, the first customers of the day came in just then: one mom with four kids, and she shushed the baby and set it into the grocery cart's child holder, legs dangling through the metal. Cade was happy it was early enough that the metal carts hadn't seen sunlight—developed a temperature hot enough to scald a rhinoceros.

"May I help you, ma'am?"

"Yeah," she said out of the corner of her mouth. "I'm looking for diapers and watermelon."

"These just came off the truck last night," Cade beamed at the large stack of seedless, oval-shaped fruit. "They're ripe . . . juicy."

"And seedless?" she inquired. "I don't want any of my babies choking on a seed," she said, face stern, appraising Cade's eyes.

"Seedless. Yes. And *ripe,*" he tried to reiterate. But she just turned and grabbed one from the side of the container and stomped toward the hygiene aisle.

She kept the children moving, and only swatted at a boy who looked a lot like a younger version of Quinn. The boy fidgeted with the grocery cart, trying to knock the baby loose from her ride.

"Stop it, Dan," she scolded. Then, she struck his wrist, and he recoiled. The boy rejoined the single file line, and they disappeared around the mouth rinse endcap.

***

Florence reappeared and took her place at the store's front. She sat beside the lotto tickets, returned merchandise bins, and maps of Seton. He didn't think a map was necessary to detail the one two-lane street going into and out of town. All 581 people resided outside the main drag. Beyond Mercer's Pub and the Seton Post Office, there was a consignment shop which simply read 'Consignment Shop,' due to switching ownership nonstop through the years. Then, there was the Seton Police Department and a sign saying: *Thanks for visiting!* Cade looked at the maps, figured they'd have Cumberland Lake and Spoonbill Dam as well. Tourism was the only source of revenue anyways.

"Want one?" Florence asked, seeing his eyes boring into the wall of maps.

"I'm fine. Just didn't know those were there."

"They've been hanging so long the grit is settled all over 'em," she said, shaking one off and dusting it open.

Cade heard the brochure *crinkle.* He laughed at the atavistic look of the town outline. Then, he frowned. It wasn't much different to its present state. The map read 1978 in the corner. The smell wasn't good. *None of it was.*

Then, the automatic doors were triggered open and in walked Paulie for first shift, bags prominent under both eyes. "Yo, fellas," he said. "How's it feel to see me after dinner and before breakfast?"

"I've felt better," Florence answered. She put the map down on the counter, trying to refold it the best she could—its resistance evident by the sounds it made.

Suddenly, the phone rang. It rang, and Paulie looked to Cade. "Get it, boss man!" He crept like a sloth to the back office to retrieve his meat department apron—blood stains and sanitizer still showing from yesterday's mess, Cade imagined.

"Get a new apron!" Florence barked at him, when he reappeared.

The phone wasn't letting up, and the Bigsby Food Market didn't have an answering machine. Another setback for a short-staffed business, Cade thought. He noted the fifteen or so patrons shopping inside already, and said, "Here, help them." Cade handed the keys for the money tills to Florence. "I'll be right back."

"Mr. Rainy, you're not playing by the rules," she chided, as he found the phone in the manager's office.

"Hello. Thanks for dialing Seton's own Bigsby Food Market! How can I help?" he said automatically, his big, fake grin held tight for no one to see.

"Oh. Hi. Yeah, can I speak to Cade?" a tired, familiar voice asked. "Is he in yet?"

Cade recognized the voice faintly; he could picture the aloofness of the person asking for him.

"Hello? I'm looking for Cade. C-a-d-e," the caller spelled, laughing at his own joke. "Just get him for me. Tell him it's Santa Claus calling to give him his summer naughty/nice check-up."

"Quinn? Hey! I thought it was you. Yeah, it's me!" Cade said, his grin holding, his voice becoming more authentic and relaxed.

"Cade. Shoot! You coulda fooled me. You sounded like a robot or something. What're they doing to ya over there?"

And the way he said *over there* made his friend feel a million miles away. Cade gripped the phone receiver away from his body and leaned to look out the swinging doors—more customers bustled into the Unhealthy Aisle. They seemed to be multiplying exponentially. "Listen, bud. I don't have a lot of time." Cade exhaled. "What's happenin'? How are things in Bowling Green?"

"What are they doin' to you? Making you run laps around the building? Ya sound wiped."

"You could say that again. It's summer, and get this . . . Clip's out sick. Indefinitely."

"Bill Clip's out? Dang, man. That stinks. Who's running the show then?"

"You know who."

"Oh snap! They have you doing Bill Clip's work and yours?"

"And about three other peoples' too. Short-handed as always."

"Manager Rainy of the Bigsby Food Market? Look at you, kid. On to bigger and well, I was about to say better things. But, I digress."

"I only have a sec. This is all still so new. It's pure torture, man. I don't know if I—"

Quinn cleared his throat. Silence fell over the line, and Cade wanted him to say something. Tell him how the move to WKU was going. Anything to make the day better. "Listen, there's a *real* reason I'm calling, and I think you're going to like it . . ."

"Go on. You know I don't have time for games. Paulie will accidentally stab himself if he's left alone too long," Cade said, holding his breath in the stale, cigarette-smoky air.

"Okay. Well, you know I'm an adventurer like you. I pride myself on years of saving your sorry hide in the caves of southern Kentucky."

"Is there a point to this story, or are you calling to gloat? C'mon."

"There's a point. And it's this. Since we were eighth graders, you've been forcing me and Mercedes to come along with you on these expeditions. Right?"

"What're you saying?"

"WKU is putting together these sweet trips to the mother of all caves: Mammoth! Led by college students! I know you have your *responsibilities* to Clip and all, but this is your ticket, man. If you don't take it, well, I'm not sure we can ever speak again," his voice teased, but there was a seriousness also.

Cade felt the realness of the option. Just for a moment. *Quinn wouldn't mess with me about this!* He turned the phone's earpiece outward and looked at it. His hands were clammy and shaking all of a sudden.

"Cade. You still there?" Quinn's voice boomed. "Talk to me. I have to tell them by today. The park guide seemed really excited to meet you."

Cade stretched the cord out again, peered through the tar-streaked, smoky glass again and saw a mom wrestling a seedless melon away from her child.

Then, Paulie burst in through the swinging doors. "Cade, it's getting wild. There's a family wanting short ribs and they want 'em a quarter-inch thick." He hung his head. "I can't do a quarter-inch. You know that."

It was an ongoing hatred of Mr. Elway's, his, and Paulie's to cut the beef short ribs so slim. There was always a high risk of losing a finger. Jerry Sarkins had lost one just a few weeks back, and he went away in the back of an ambulance. No one had seen him since.

"Hel-lo?! Cade? If you don't want to go, just say N-O. That's all I want. Just a simple no," Quinn said through the phone's earpiece. "But you'll regret it forever. They said they would even train us."

"Who's that?" Paulie asked.

"Paulie, do the best you can and tell them to wait. Mr. Elway will be in in about fifteen minutes. Or so the schedule says. Tell the family he'll cut them, because I don't want you ending up like Sarkins. Losing your entire arm or worse. Okay?"

"Got it, boss man," he said, knocking the doors back open, exiting like a cool kid.

"This trip. Is it all summer?"

"There you are, buddy. Why are you being so—"

"Just listen, Quinn. Is it?"

"The rest of summer and paid, too. It's more like a tour guide thing. We'll be the ones in charge, according to the letter I got. Plus, there'll be ladies."

"And they'd want me to lead and that's it?" he asked, heart racing. "Even though I'm not in college?"

Florence entered the manager's office, said, "I can't take it, Cade. You've been back here longer than I was. You're the manager. Get out there and tell those moms there's a limit. Four melons per family."

"Florence, er, Flo. Don't take this the wrong way, but today is going to be *it*."

"Come again?" she asked, voice husky. "Good one, young man."

Cade held the phone back to his ear once more. "Quinn, tell them I'll be over there to get you at WKU ASAP."

"All right, my man! I'll tell them everything. And don't worry about—"

Cade set the phone back into its cradle, Quinn still talking, and walked past Florence—her mouth agape. He paused long enough to hang his apron on the wall hook.

"But you can't leave! You're Clip's replacement until he gets back . . . you're . . . you're *responsible*."

Cade didn't pause, but continued down Aisle 14, where he picked up a bag of Cheetos, and then, snatched a map of Seton—for nostalgia's sake. He did think to lay a couple of dollars on the counter—to pay for the Cheetos—so there wouldn't be a shortage later. He admitted he felt bad about not having enough to pay for Mr. Lobster; but he imagined Mr. Lobster was store inventory for so long it no longer mattered, or affected the budget that much. Then, he dug deeper into his pocket and left all the small bills (and change he had on him) which came to about ten dollars.

He inhaled the Citronella candles affixed to the wooden torches at the store's exit. The thought of the *Adventure* that awaited him and his best friend made him smile.

# CHAPTER FIFTEEN

The Rainy home was empty when Cade entered.

The coffee mug Abbott often used set unwashed on the table, and his mom's laundry still tumbled in the dryer. The timer went off, and he removed the hot sheets and quilt. When he clicked the door shut, he saw his mom through the washroom's window, picking blackberries from one of the bushes surrounding the edge of their field. She held a bucket and waved her finger in the air like she'd been bitten.

Cade trudged out to the fence's edge to see what was wrong. He saw her fingers stained a dark purple from all of the berries she'd picked and put into the bucket. Her hand was cut from the thorns. "Mom?"

"Oh, Cade. These darn berries are getting the best of me. I took off work to do this, before Abbott sprayed around his lot later today. Now, I've officially broken my pride." She laughed, pinching a thorn from her index finger. "You're home early. Tell me it's good news," she said, scratching her nose gently with her thumb.

"It is if you look at the glass half full."

"Okay. That's the look of a Rainy in trouble, if I've ever seen one." Her face was light, smiling still. "What's going on?"

"I spoke with Quinn about an hour ago . . ."

"He's back from Bowling Green already? I thought he was out there all summer, before college started up?"

"He is. See, that's why he was calling. He wants—"

"Cade, I wish we had the means to send you off to school properly, but you know we can't afford it. Just like Mercedes at UK. We'd love to send you, but it's just too much," she added.

"It's not that, Mom," he said. "I know you do."

"It's not college?" she asked, her brow raised. "Then what is it?"

"He told me about this job over in western Kentucky. It's tied to Mammoth Cave, and the WKU people get to serve as tour guides . . . and they get paid. They invited me."

The words impacted Hollie, he could tell. She set the blackberries down, turned Cade's shoulders with both her hands and looked at him closely. "Mammoth Cave, hmm?" she asked, holding the words closely inside the roof of her mouth like they meant something more, her voice quivering a little, too.

"The biggest and best cave," Cade said, trying to restrain his giddiness but doing a poor job.

"I know where Mammoth is," she said too fast. "What about Bigsby? Didn't you say Mr. Clip was out indefinitely, because of some illness? Wouldn't this be leaving them stranded?"

"Flo is the HR person. She's responsible for all of the hiring and firing. If she wanted to, she could bring in three more people tomorrow. She needs to, it being summer and all. I told her that, but she wouldn't listen. Now, she'll have to get help, because—"

"Because you're going?" she asked, answering his heart more than his words.

"Th-that's right. If you'll allow it."

Hollie stared at his chest, into what felt like his very soul. How did she do that? She turned his cheek from side to side and analyzed his posture. After a few minutes of inspection, she let him go, scooped her bucket back from the ground and commenced picking well-hidden, juicy berries. Cade followed suit and did his best to add to her stockpile. They picked for several minutes in silence, and suddenly they heard a horse whinny.

Cade looked and saw Abbott riding Clay—the large, brown beast tossing his head and blowing air out his nostrils.

"Hullo, neighbors," he said fondly. "Glad you got to these berries before I turned the pesticides loose. I hated to rush you, but the tobacco won't suffer under those bugs much longer. I remember when bugs were pesky but never this way," he said, spitting juice from his mouth.

"You're lucky my work lets people off to go pick berries in the middle of the day," she teased, turning to face the wild-looking, white-haired man.

"Cade. You're a rare sight this time of day. They must be letting new managers work when they feel like it at Bigsby. That right?"

"Not a manager anymore, Abbott. I let myself *go*," Cade answered quietly.

"Let yourself go? That sounds like a really bad movie title. What do you mean? They thought operating without a manager was a good idea? I'm going to have to go talk some sense into that niece of mine, Flo. She doesn't have the sense God gave a jackrabbit."

"She's fine," Cade countered. "I just decided it was time I moved into something a little bit more . . . me."

"You?" Abbott asked. "What's more you?"

Cade looked to his mom, and she turned back to the berries, wiping the water from her eyes with her blouse sleeve. Her voice shook as she said, "Cade's found an *opportunity* to be a cave guide. He got a call from Quinsey Bates earlier. And he's got his heart set on going out to Mammoth Cave and making a little extra money. Ain't that right?" she asked, her back still turned, hiding something else Cade felt.

He nodded slowly. "I want to see how big, how different Mammoth is to *our* cave. I've heard it's the biggest in the world. Quinn said it'll be the chance of a lifetime."

Abbott spat again, stepped down from Clay using his stirrup. He took the reins over the horse's head and led the gelding up close, where he fed the ornery horse a blackberry or two.

"Those are for us," Hollie said, a forced smile forming on her face.

Abbott returned her gaze and she offered a berry from the bowl. Cade watched and didn't mind his mom's affection for Abbott. He was one of the best men he'd met in Seton—apart from Dad, of course. He was one of the good things that had happened to them.

"Well, when do you head out, young man?"

"We haven't decided yet," Hollie said, jerking the bowl away again.

"He has to go to Mammoth. It's over four hundred miles of caves," he said, gloved hands flapping the air, startling Clay.

"You've been?" Cade asked, excitement rising again.

"Lots of times. There are so many great expeditions out there. It's something!"

And Abbott's excitement made Cade even more on edge. *Why didn't Mom want it?* Her gaze remained on the blackberry bushes.

He tugged on her sleeve, and she finally looked at him. "What, Cade?" she said, no longer trying to fight back tears. "You're a grown man now."

"If you don't want me to, all you have to say is that. I won't go. But, if you do say it's okay, I'll be sure to leave soon."

"Considerate and everything. What about that?" Abbott added, keeping the gelding away from the berry bowl. "He'll bite your hand off, Hollie, if you don't watch him. Clay will, not Cade," he kidded.

Hollie looked at the horse and then to Cade. "Is that what you really want? More than the Bigsby manager job?"

"You know it is. I want an *Adventure*, Mom. Quinn will keep me in line," he added, knowing she wouldn't believe it.

She pulled him close, and the berry bowl almost toppled out of her hand. Abbott got to it just in time, smacking Clay with the reins. "Quit it, boy," he scolded. "Do you want to founder and die?"

"You better help me with these, because I know what I'm making. Since you're heading off to no man's land. I'll have to make a proper dessert," she said to Cade, defeat in her voice and a tinge of pain, too.

"No man's land," Cade laughed, squeezing her hard and releasing her. "I thought that's where we were standing now: Seton, Kentucky. No? I've got a map from the market to prove it."

Abbott enjoyed the humor, because he spat out his tobacco plug and scooped up a handful of ripe berries. "That's right, Hollie. What's more country" (which sounded like *cantry)* "than good ole Seton, *Kay Why*? Full of misfits and miscreants." He laughed, grabbing Clay's reins and burying the horse's face in the berries. The gelding didn't resist.

"Now, I already told you fellas not to waste the berries. I'm going to bake something."

Cade's spirits rose. He knew what that meant, and he missed the taste like he missed the company of his closest friends. *Blackberry cobbler!*

"That's right," Hollie nodded, watching Cade's reaction, his recognition. "But, only if he keeps that horse away, and you get in here and risk your life against critters and vermin instead of me."

Cade took the bucket, as Hollie stepped back and spoke with Abbott quietly about something, some memory she had. He reached into the bushes and extracted the biggest, sweetest pieces he could find. He remembered Dad and Mom picking the larger ones—claiming they were sweeter than the smaller, more compact ones. He sampled both and had to agree the tinier pieces were tart like a persimmon.

Cade snacked on a few and filled the bucket in twice the time it took Hollie to fill it halfway. When he was bleeding from the thorns and sweating properly, he stepped back from a bush loaded with beetles, spiders, and bumblebees. "Why does everything love blackberries?"

"Even the snakes," Abbott answered. "You gotta watch out for the snakes. They like the sweet ones."

At this, Cade jumped back from the edge of the thorns and tore another gash in his forearm. "Youch!"

"Watch it! You'll end up just like a friend of mine who lived here once. Broken-hearted and hungry, if you don't watch yourself in those *haunted* briars," Abbott confided.

Cade had never heard him talk about who owned the land before. He waited for more backstory, but Abbott didn't divulge any. "So . . .?" Cade finally said.

"Moving away from us and you still want a story free of charge. Do I have it right?"

Cade nodded. "Tell me about these people. Uncivilized and backward like us lake folk?" he jested, feeling good about the future for once.

"I think I have time for a brief recollection of the former tenants, if you have some money," he said, holding out his hand.

"I don't have a job," Cade admitted. "As of today, I'm unemployed."

"If I heard right, you have a new one starting next week. So, I can be paid later, I guess," Abbott withdrew his hand. "IOUs work just fine."

"Roger that. I'll pay when the cave money shows up," Cade said. "Now go on. What's with this land? Is it sacred Cherokee burial ground? Did you know a millionaire who struck oil? What?"

Cade waited for him to begin; he crossed his arms impatiently, hoping it would get Abbott started.

"The family before you all were the Vandersons. This was the *Vandersons' Place*. All fifty acres. Exact same layout. Except they did something that the government doesn't know about and probably won't ever. See, they bought this land from the Seton Courthouse in the 1890s, and raised a whole brood of children here."

Cade scooted closer to Abbott. He gave the bowl to Hollie's outstretched hand.

"I better get this dessert cooking," she said, kissing Cade's forehead gently, walking to the back porch, and entering the ranch house.

"The family was growing bigger and bigger. I heard tell that there were fifteen of them at one point, not counting their dad and mom. Anyways, one day one or two of the bigger kids were outside playing in the field, and they were climbing and doing like children do. Then, one of the older boys climbs up on what he thinks is a bale of hay, because it's covered by grass, and it rests beside the other bales. How the family never knew these were there, I don't know. But anyways, the boy climbs up and begins to jump onto the next bale of hay, and when he does, the grass comes off the surface, and the kids can see beneath. The boy supposedly cleaned the debris away, and what do you think was there?"

Cade's mouth was open; he loved the way Abbott told a story.

"It was a small Confederate cemetery. Four soldiers. A family of them. Three brothers and a father. The father's tombstone was a little bit bigger, and it was a general's monument. All of them had been covered up and overlooked for ages. Then, when the dad of this Vanderson Brady Bunch returned home, the oldest boy went to him, saying, "Dad, we found something," and he showed the man. Rather than congratulate the boy and tell someone, the old man went and retrieved his tractor. Supposedly, he hooked the headstones to a strong chain and hauled all of them out to the big sinkhole—the entrance to your cave. The man is rumored to have tossed all of them down into the darkness to remain a mystery forever, covering the cave's entrance up and forcing his kids to never speak of it. And somehow, the story goes that the kids didn't." Abbott shook his head. "I still don't know how fifteen kids kept quiet, but maybe the old man threatened their lives. Whatever the means it's said that this land is still haunted by those four soldiers to this day." Abbott exhaled, his story ended.

Cade was afraid to move. "How in the world? I've never seen any abandoned tombstones, and I've been down there hundreds of times with M! The cave's empty," he heard himself say to Abbott's back, as the old man walked the gelding up the hill and mounted him.

"It might be empty, or, you might've overlooked it."

"No way!"

"Very well. Giddyup," Abbott said to his gelding. "I'll see you for blackberries in a little bit, huh?"

Cade entered the house and found his mom swaying to a Percy Sledge song—a favorite of Dad's she hadn't played in years. He washed his hands, offering to help while his mind traveled down Highway 90, rocketing fast toward Mammoth Cave.

# CHAPTER SIXTEEN

"Take it! You drive it more than I do anyways," Abbott said, kicking the pickup's tires.

And it was decided just like that. Cade thanked the old man for the truck; he kissed his mom. Hollie was beside herself. Cade reasoned that only the essentials should go into the Ford. The life he knew was formed by God and largely the two people now in front of him. He heard himself say, "Take care of that gelding!"

Abbott shouted he would, over the truck's rumble-grumble idling.

"Don't get too close to *strangers,*" Mom said, leaning into the driver's side of the cab—kissing him again, her eyes soaking his shirt. "You make this trip a special one, and tell Quinn to take care of you, or I'll box his ears."

Cade thought the words were odd and comical coming from his mom. "What in the world? I figured that kind of language from Mize, but not you, Mom." He smiled and kissed her one more time. "Besides, I can take care of Quinn better than he can himself."

"You're right. Bring yourself back safe and sound, you hear?"

Abbott tapped the truck bed a couple of times with his knuckles. He cleared his throat. "When you see the blind, albino cave shrimp make a wish. They're good luck."

Even in his departure, Abbott was still unbelievable. "I'll do just that."

"They're endangered and exotic just like me." His deep voice bellowed a loud laugh. "Tell Quinn he's an Eskimo," Abbott added, shutting the truck door all the way.

"Goodbye," Cade said, then adjusted his driver-side mirror and shifted into drive. The truck rattled forward and lurched a little bit.

"Love you, son," Hollie said. He saw her, and Abbott Mize, in the rearview mirror all the way onto Highway 90—into the first part of the descent toward Seton.

***

Fueling up at the E-Z pump and grabbing a bite at Smitty's before he left was a great idea. With his stomach settled somewhat, he was able to focus on the open road. Cade waved one final time at the people on the streets of Seton. The crazy old townie, Sam Sanders, or Snoops as he was affectionately known, sat on the Seton Post Office steps and waved as Cade went by. The porch outside Mercer's Pub was vacant, and Cade felt delight in knowing he would be working alongside Mercer's nephew, Quinsey Bates, soon enough. He tipped his hat to the Bigsby twins, and some regulars at the Consignment Shop. Then, he passed the Bigsby Food Market and saw a scenario he'd hoped would never resurface. The same dark, grimy, swarthy man from the previous day loped out the main entrance with another haul of filet mignon packages. Cade saw Paulie swatting at him with a broom, bloodstains everywhere on his work apron. Just behind them, Flo was chasing with a cigarette tucked between her lips, her cell phone out dialing the cops. Cade didn't even try to duck the spectacle, but rather, he waved and honked the mournful truck's horn as he passed the storefront.

The truck bucked and dipped around the corners heading out of town. The 581 citizens would have to fare on their own without him. Make that 580, he thought. He saw the speed limit posted at the county line as 55 MPH. Cade pushed the accelerator down to the floor and watched the RPM and speedometer gauges climb.

The smaller communities were Cade's favorites. He'd appreciated the unique names of the communities east of Monticello, pronounced Monti-sell-o. In this order they were: *Number One, Slat, Susie, Alpha, Snow, Marrowbone, Willow Shade, Summer Shade, and Eighty-Eight*. Eighty-Eight, and its quaint, quiet streets were like something from a Steven Spielberg film in the 1980s. Eighty-Eight was also the last community on his family's trips between Seton and Glasgow, Kentucky. Once they arrived at this intersection, it was a connection to the Cumberland Parkway and Interstate 65, before exiting to Bowling Green.

Even the name of the Cumberland Parkway triggered thoughts of the lake and what he was leaving behind. The Spoonbill Dam, he admitted, was something he'd never fully shake from his memory. It was forever linked to Dad, and he was with him wherever he went. The traffic around Cade picked up; he merged cautiously onto I-65.

***

Cade turned down a street leading to campus, and he called Quinn's cell. The phone rang three times and his friend picked up. "You out front?" the deep, familiar voice asked.

"You know it."

"Get your game face on. We're driving separate from the larger group today. I told our team leader we'd be there earlier than the rest."

Cade said fine. He hung up, and the two left when Quinn was inside the Ford's cab. Quinn was somehow larger in size than just weeks prior, when they'd graduated. Now, he seemed a bulky mass of muscles hunched over in the passenger side of the truck. He raised a Cheshire grin toward Cade.

"Don't distract me while I'm driving. You know it could send both of us to the morgue."

"Mammoth Cave. We have to backtrack a little toward Glasgow, amigo. We'll go past Smith's Grove where Abbott bought that gelding, and we'll turn at Park City. All in all, we're looking at thirty minutes, give or take," Quinn said, stroking his two-day-old stubble.

"You been living in the gym or what?" Cade asked. "Protein supplements much?"

Quinn checked himself out in the mirror; he looked to Cade and gave a smug head nod. "The girls are going to notice this fall," he beamed.

Cade teased him, saying that being in a cave all summer wasn't a great way to see the beauties at WKU or be seen. The thought sobered Quinn, and he fell silent for the remainder of the drive. When they entered Mammoth Cave National Park, Cade breathed deeply. To him, even the air smelled cleaner than it did back home. Cade shifted the gear to park, clicked the key off. He stretched his arms and longed for a Red Bull—the only purchase he'd make at the Bigsby while working his old shifts.

"You're licking your lips like a Brahma bull," Quinn said. "You see some girl I missed?"

Cade loved Quinn's ability to make any conversation light-hearted. His exceptional confidence was contagious. Cade remembered their years of exploring the caves. While M had always been with him, Cade had even seen M smile a time or two at Quinn's efforts to woo her.

"Right in front of Cade? Really?" she'd blurted, and the cave echoed her surprise.

Quinn said, "If you see an eight or a nine today, let me know. Seven or below, I'm good to pass."

Cade remembered the ten-point scale his friend always used; he smiled knowing it was still in full effect at Western. "10-4, good buddy," he responded. "I'll be your wing man. Even in a cave, I guess."

The two laughed and Quinn sang his heart out to a *Black Keys* song on the radio. Cade started to buy admissions tickets to the national park, and his friend stopped him. "Whoa there! We're guests—and future workers—in these labyrinthine caves. Our dinero is no good here, okay?"

Cade slipped the twenty back into his money clip. Bill Clip came to mind, and he laughed.

"Honestly. The price is already covered," Quinn added.

Cade shook his head in agreement. The two scoped out the gift shop and waited for the main park guide they were supposed to meet, Joshua King.

The shop was extremely busy, and the summer season was in full swing. Cade picked up souvenirs, inspected them, and set them cautiously back in their places. The prices were high, but so was *everything* outside Seton. His hands grew clammy in anticipation of the guide's arrival. "How old's Joshua?"

"He's about your mom's age, I guess," Quinn said. "Why?"

"Just curious. Does he know the caves? All of them?"

His best friend looked at the items in the shop and back to Cade. "He says he does, and I believe him. Anytime there's an expedition here he's on it . . . or, so I'm told. Joshua King is a household name around here."

"He's seen the creatures in the River Styx?" Cade pried.

"I bet you he's named the wooly worms one by one."

The gift shop attendant looked in their direction and gave her best, *It's not a library, but I appreciate the use of the inside voice,* face. The two acquiesced to her request and spoke in quieter tones—a real feat for Quinn's deep voice.

The bell above the door jingled, and both heads turned. In walked a man in his late forties carrying a climber's pack, his blue eyes piercing. He held the gift shop worker's hand politely, and said, "Doris, thank you for being the best worker in the entire park! I love seeing your face each day." Then, he walked over to Quinn and Cade, scratching at the long beard on his face. With the same amount of enthusiasm—like a teenager, Cade thought, he said, "Quinsey Bates, welcome to heaven on earth. They said you'd be here early . . . and this must be your co-navigator? Our special guest this summer."

Quinn stared at the man much the same way Cade did, then said, "This is him . . . Cade Rainy. Best cave spelunker in southeast Kentucky. He's Seton's pride and joy!"

The man took in Cade and placed his hands on the teen's shoulders. His blue eyes looked up and down Cade's frame. Normally, it would've unnerved him for someone to do this, even Quinn—history and all. But, for some reason, this man's confidence was intoxicating. He stood still, until the man offered his hand to Cade. He took it, said, "Cade Rainy."

"You ready to set a course for our thrill-seekers this summer?" he asked.

"I'm just happy to be here," Cade offered, afraid of failing any preliminary test.

"Joshua King," he finally offered. "I've been in Mammoth a long time. Not a day goes by that I don't find some little bit of terrain that's completely new. Look at us. I've already found you. The streak continues. With endless miles to search, it goes without saying that it's almost without overlap, never boring. Shall we get you all suited up for the first *express* tour?"

Neither spoke. Cade and Quinn gawked at his enthusiasm, his sense of purpose. Finally, Quinn found his voice and said, "Lead on, Mr. King."

Joshua King turned, and without further instruction, exited the gift shop. Cade set down a glass figurine he had been inspecting and followed the man's course.

# CHAPTER SEVENTEEN

Joshua King led them into the Visitor Center. He picked up a newspaper with weather forecasts for the next week. He said, "I only trust the one that says today's date," over his shoulder. "Weather changes too fast for someone in a cave to take risks. You know we're just a few hours from the epicenter of the New Madrid fault line?"

Cade looked at Quinn for an explanation but none came. He stared blankly at Mr. King and waited for him to continue. King said nothing else about it, and walked through the center to the back of the building. Here, he tossed each a booklet. "Read up. I expect my guides to be more knowledgeable than this author." Then, he flicked a black, moleskin journal at Cade. "This one is especially for you, ranger. It's special." He winked oddly. "I couldn't find what I was looking for. Maybe you can and when you do, let me know."

Both teens opened their booklets. Cade read: *Spelunkers Guide, 2014.* He flipped through the booklet and saw terminology that he, Quinn, and M had used on a more rudimentary level throughout high school.

"That there is the finest bite-sized information on caving you'll find anywhere," Joshua King said. "All the terms and the maneuvering you'll need from now through the end of August, start of September. 'Kay?"

Quinn didn't answer, but Cade looked up and said, "Sure thing." His eyes mulled over the glossary; he landed on a term which jolted him fully awake. "Hey, Mr. King? I see a *fissure cave* listed. Do we have to go through a lot of these, or—"

"*You* will. And sooner than you think. Glad you asked. It won't be a problem, will it?"

"No, sir," Cade answered.

"Joshua is fine. You don't have to salute me, or anything." He laughed, his eyes holding a familiar gaze on Cade.

Did he know him from somewhere?

Quinn flipped through the book and shut it abruptly. "I know this already, Joshua. Been there done that. You know we aren't rookies. Are we, Cade? Can we just take a refresher course and be on our way?"

Joshua shook his head. "No chance. You'll study that book and memorize it forward and back. Then, you'll report to me on how to use it to save someone else's life." His tone was even, his smile intact.

Cade wished Bill Clip possessed this ability to teach, while remaining calm.

"Are there any other concerns I need to know about?"

"Concerns?" Quinn snickered. "What . . . like fears?"

"Well, like the fissure cave. I'd put that in the fear column, since he brought it up."

"Cade's a little bit afraid of a lot of things. Aren't you, Rainy? But, he's a quick learner." Quinn slapped him on the shoulder with a meaty paw.

Cade shook him off. "I'm not a huge fan of water," he admitted, trying to keep thoughts of dark pools of water from distracting him.

"Not a huge fan of water. I like that." Joshua laughed. "Well, that's one we better cure fast, because there's a ton of it at Mammoth. The Green River is a tributary, and the Styx River runs throughout the cave system. So we better figure it out. What ails you?" His eyes still looked like they knew something, squinting and bird-like.

"Cade lost his dad, like I told you earlier," Quinn interrupted, coming to his friend's aid.

"He can tell me himself," Joshua reprimanded.

Cade closed the book momentarily and looked between his friend and the guide. He felt around inside his head for words—a headache forming. When he looked back to Joshua, he said, "My dad was an underwater welder in Seton . . . worked on Spoonbill Dam. He was a coal miner before that."

"I see." Joshua picked up the trailing thought. "And, he was with you on Cumberland Lake the last time you saw him?"

"Right. How'd you know that?"

"Well, it seems the water is a definite trigger, and I can see why. Aquaphobia is more common than you'd think," he added. "There are varying degrees."

"Aquaphobia?" Quinn said.

"I'm not afraid of water like that," Cade started to argue. "I can swim and stuff, but—"

"You just don't want to be around it, if you can help it?"

Cade nodded his head, remembering the first time Quinn and M jumped in the watering hole inside their cave.

"Well, that fear has to stop," he said flatly. "Not just subverted or distracted. It has to be removed from your subconscious while you spelunk."

Cade didn't move.

"Has to. Otherwise, you're putting others' well-being at risk—because they need to be lucid and in control while you help them move across the cave. So, that's a no-brainer. If you're calm, you can keep others safe."

"But—"

"End of discussion. Fear has to go. A-W-A-Y," he spelled out.

Cade looked to his friend. Quinn held his chin cupped inside his big palm.

"And what about you, big fella?" Joshua asked. "What gets your goat?"

"Not a thing, my man. Not one thing. Not even bats."

"There has to be something," Joshua said.

"Okay. There is one thing, but you're gonna give me grief, if I say it."

"We're not here to make your life easy," Joshua chided.

"Fine. It's not bats, but . . . their crap. Guano. I can't stand the thought of it on me," Quinn added, shaking his shoulders like it was on him.

"Wait . . . wait." Joshua laughed. "You're not afraid of bats, but you're afraid of their poop?"

Quinn held up his hand. "It drops down from above you. Doesn't that bother you, man?"

"No more than any other critter pooping on me," Joshua said.

Cade laughed, feeling relieved the pressure was off him for the moment.

"You and Quinsey have some light reading before we go out. But, like I said, it's essential that your fears are gone, and you're well-read. I want the best guides imaginable. Why do you think I asked you two to arrive before the rest? Because I want you to *teach*. So, you have tonight to read that thing and know it inside and out," he said. "I'm talking chambers, harnesses, and blind shrimp. Every bit!"

"That's a lot of stuff! What about this one?" Cade asked, looking at the moleskin journal held together by an elastic strap. He saw Joshua's eyes land on it, and his face contorted into a tight smile, then relaxed somewhat.

"There're fissure caves like Big Man's Misery, Cade. You won't want to lose sleep over it, but it's tight. Try controlling your breathing, when you think about the real thing. It will help you develop a tad more control. Okay?" Joshua said, ignoring Cade's question.

Cade was glad he'd brought his dad's headlight and helmet. They were fastened inside the backpack slung over his shoulder. Would his dad join him in this *Expedition*, if he were alive? He imagined Haven Rainy would do anything, if dared.

"You listening, Rainy?" Quinn said.

"Hmm?"

"Joshua just told us to memorize this entire book by tomorrow. Or, it's back to the Bigsby for you." He laughed.

Cade said he would and turned to go. Thoughts of Big Man's Misery and fissure caves were filling up with rushing water inside his head. He shivered at the notion of being flooded.

"One more thing, Cade. Tomorrow we'll start early. Breakfast will be in the Visitor Center at 7:00 a.m. sharp. I can't wait to see what you and this knucklehead can do. What you can find. Good evening."

Joshua left them, and Quinn led them to where their bunks were. "Beats the heck out of my dorm room at Western," he mouthed.

Cade placed his sleeping bag on top of the top bunk. He was rooming with Quinn, and they were *Explorers* again. Excitement propelled him to smack Quinn's back. It made a loud *pop!* and he realized he'd swung too hard.

"Geez! Rainy!"

Cade laughed and climbed to the top bunk. He sprawled out and perused the booklet. He saw familiar terms like: *true north, stalactite,* and *erosion*. What amazed Cade was how a subject like biology had bored him to tears in high school, and here, in nature, he loved how those things blended with real life. Mathematics could never do this. There were labyrinths and caverns large enough to fit Boeing 747s, and he smiled at the magnificence of what lay below the ground.

Then he came to the term *stream bed* and halted again. It depicted water as running over a cave surface. The image was unsettling, and he shut the book.

"You gonna be all right?" Quinn asked, turning from the windowsill.

Cade shrugged his shoulders. "I have to be, I guess. I'm here at Mammoth, aren't I?"

"No turning back now, buddy. Besides, I have your back. Imagine how much confidence you're gonna have when we tell Mercedes. She'll flip her lid, when she knows you conquered this one."

"She knows I can swim a little. I told her about Abbott taking me to Cumberland."

"I know, but this is below ground again. You've never jumped into water in a . . ." he thumbed through the glossary, 'a subterranean environment.' " He laughed.

"No, I haven't. First time for everything," Cade agreed. "What about Big Man's Misery? Think I can get through it?"

"No question. Thousands of people are claustrophobic. I've met a few on-campus who can't stand being in a crowded elevator. Can you imagine how they'd freak in a cave?"

"They wouldn't even get on a plane, I bet," Cade said.

"Let alone a cave that could crush them with one burp from the tectonic plates shifting below ground," Quinn added.

"Too far," Cade said. "I didn't need that image."

"What do you think King was talking about when he mentioned the New Madrid fault?"

Cade paused and tried to remember. It was in Fulton County, Kentucky, Ms. Easter had said once. It was where the main disaster would start, if a big earthquake ever hit the mid-west. The aftershocks would ripple all around that place in a bigger (and wider) circle. When they stretched out to Mammoth Cave, it would be like breaking a pretzel stick—if it was the earth's crust above the cave. *Crash!*

Quinsey sat down on the bottom bunk and mulled over his terminology for a few quiet moments.

Cade breathed out and thumbed through the glossary and delved into the harnessing techniques and the grid of Mammoth's 400 miles below ground. How could it be that huge? He shifted on the twin bed mattress and felt the moleskin journal beneath his ribcage. When he'd extracted it, he unwrapped the elastic band and opened the journal to its first page, remembering King's avoidance to his question.

He read:

> *This journal is the property of Haven Rainy, Adventurer to the Max! 1982. If you find this piece of gold, return it to me ASAP! Thanks so much.*

Cade's hands shook, and he accidentally dropped the journal on his bed. He peered out the window. *No flipping way!! There's no possible way!*

But he reopened it and saw the penmanship. The usage of capital letters on words like *Adventurer* and *Max* were too coincidental. His mouth hung open for a full minute.

"He knows Dad!" he heard himself shout, hopping off the bed and forcing the first page into Quinn's face. "Look. Dad knew Mr. King."

"If you'd stop waving it around, I might be able to see whatever it is you're saying," Quinn spat, closing his spelunking booklet. "What's your dad got to do with Joshua?"

"Check it out!" Cade opened the journal again, hands trembling. "See the name, the date? That's Dad all right. And see," he said, pointing to the return address. "King was playing us like dummies!" He laughed.

"That's odd," Quinn offered. He reached for the moleskin, but Cade pushed his burly hand away.

The two sat down on the bottom bunk, and Cade flipped the journal open to the first page and ran his fingers over the slightly grooved font. *Dad must've pressed down hard with the pen, for it to be so indented.* "He calls it his piece of gold," he pointed out to Quinn again.

"It's like a gift from beyond the grave, ain't it? Why'd King have it?"

Cade hardened, turned his shoulder away. The notion of his father dead still bothered him. It might always be that way, he figured. Cade stood and climbed to the top bunk again.

"Fine," Quinn argued. "I need to know this book anyways," he said. "And, it's not going to stick by osmosis. I learned that much at Seton High. I don't need to be snooping in another man's journal anyways," his tone jocular.

"Stay down there," Cade remarked. Unable to control his giddiness, he pried the binding open again, and the spine creaked where the glue had stiffened over the years. Had anyone seen this since '82? Except King? It was in his possession. But the noise of the creaky spine made him wonder. Without any other reservation, he delved into it.

***

*22 September 1982*

*The Historic Entrance plummets downward. It's rugged and wild like the hills of Cobank. I don't miss Seton and family though, because the cave pulls me into itself. The concrete steps and touristy entrance doesn't cheapen the opening either. Everyone has to get down to the cave floor. You have to start at the floor of any Adventure! Me and King are starting our spelunking and hoping to help the crews at Mammoth find new ground. It's an Explorer's Paradise!*

*Head lamp on,*<br>*Haven*

*P.S. I was told by a certain someone (Hollie Johnston) that we had to say we missed Cumberland. This is me saying I miss home . . . not!!*

Cade shut the journal again and discovered something else, his mom's maiden name. *She was with Dad and King once.*

"Quinn! Quinn! Check this out!" he said, reaching the journal down.

"I thought we weren't talking. You need to be studying, Rainy," he argued. "I'm not the only one who needs to be ready—"

"Just read it," Cade urged. "Read the first entry," he said. "See it?"

"I'm reading. Reading. Okay. Got it," he said, matter-of-factly. "They were here together," his voice cold, distant. "So what?"

"No. Not just her. See," he pressed, his hand stretching to point at the words on the faded, yellowing page. "Here? It was Dad, Mom, and King. All three. Right where we are! Crazy, huh?"

Quinn was silent. "Yeah. Neat stuff." He grunted, handing the journal above his head.

"C'mon. It *is* something. It's almost thirty years exactly, and all of them were together. I'm going to have to ask King about it tomorrow. See if he spills. He has to, because he gave me the journal. He's an old friend of Dad's. I have to get some answers. Why didn't Mom say something?" he asked.

Suddenly, the energy drained from Cade's discovery. Maybe it wasn't as cool as it felt? But, he didn't stop there. He said, "Don't you wish M was here, instead of in Lexington—training stupid horses?"

Quinn sighed loudly. He shut his booklet and thumped the underside of the bed. "Listen, Cade. She doesn't know what she's missin' and I bet she'd love a call later tonight. But, see, there might not be a *later,* if we don't learn this stuff," he said, shaking his book, the pages rustling. "Savvy?"

Cade admitted he needed to study until dinner and then later. But, his mind was abuzz. *This piece of gold.* He needed to ration his time reading it; it could be a part of his dad's legacy he'd never known about. Admitting Quinn was right, one of the few times, Cade pulled the elastic strap over the edges of the moleskin and painstakingly set it aside. He found the *Spelunkers Guide* crumpled under his knee, and he picked it up—tried to straighten it. The cover was creased, and he imagined this made it look more well-worn, well-read. It might help him tomorrow. Who knew? King might think he was studious. Then, he realized the notion was silly. The only way to prove himself to someone as capable (and connected) as Joshua King was to memorize it cover to cover. Cade let out a deep breath, as if to prepare himself for the task ahead, and reclined slowly with the book in hand. He labored over terminology familiar and foreign. He studied caving maneuvers and techniques. At one point, Cade even fished for a ballpoint pen the Visitor Center had loaned him, and took some notes in the margins of the booklet. When he shook his aching hand, he heard a buzzing cell phone sound below him, heard Quinn say, "Grub time. Let's go see what this place dines on."

Cade closed the booklet with images of a climber calling out the phrase, "That's me," to a belayer. He imagined Quinn and himself doing that very same thing soon.

# CHAPTER EIGHTEEN

Joshua King knocked on the cabin door. Both boys were up, unable to sleep much the night before. "It's time, gentlemen. Don't keep me waiting."

"Thought you said seven?" Cade groaned through the door.

"Seven a.m. ready," King confirmed. "That doesn't mean lollygagging."

"It's my fault. I asked Cade to go over the material one more time with me. It takes me a little longer than it does him," Quinn admitted.

Cade opened the cabin door, and he saw a cave guide if there ever was one. Joshua King's gear was slung over his shoulder. He looked like something out of a climber's magazine. "We're ready, Mr. Ki—er, Joshua," he said, the words spilling out.

"Gentlemen, let's hop to. You all get the first run on this maze. God's limestone labyrinth. Something spelunker Stephen Bishop called, 'grand, gloomy and peculiar,' and you'll see his meaning soon enough. Let's move!"

Cade followed King at an almost breakneck speed, with Quinn bringing up the rear.

"Did you eat? Either one of you?" King asked over his shoulder.

Cade mumbled, "*No.*"

King said, "It's gonna be a long day then. You could've used some protein for the climb."

"We can go bac—"

"Not now. Too much to do before the others get here and cloud up the trails. Listen, you two are going to be my leads on what's called *Wild Cave Tour*, okay?"

Neither moved.

"You wanted adventure, and this is your chance. Once in a lifetime. Pay close attention to what you see. Take mental notes along the way."

"Joshua, I wanted to ask you about that journal. It's from my—"

"In a bit. Right now, you need to know about *Wild Cave*. It's six hours in duration and six miles long. The cave has a lot of the fissures you were worried about, Cade. We're talking tight crawling spaces, ones where you have to get down on your hands and knees and scoot along tucked like a baby."

The two friends stared at King.

"Then, there're the ten-foot climbing walls that are freehold. You have half a day of that kind of thing. It's why we labeled it 'Extremely Strenuous' and all. Not for the faint of heart. Got it?"

Quinn nodded with more confidence than Cade felt. "We're ready," his friend mustered.

"Not even close," King teased. "These are just words now. Here, follow me."

He led them down to Mammoth Cave's main entrance past the Visitor Center—the same entrance his dad had ventured along thirty years ago. The rocks, echoes, and dripping water made Cade recall the cave on his farm.

"People lose their head in Mammoth all the time . . . no, not their literal head. But, their surroundings in the dimly lit caves. This is why it's your all's job to protect guests. First and foremost. They're your greatest responsibility. Say that back to me."

"They're our greatest responsibility." Cade matched Quinn.

"You bring them back unharmed and wowing over Mammoth, and you've done your job. Only then do you pat yourselves on the back."

Both said yes, they agreed.

"Now, let's get to what you learned last night. I only have one question for you . . ." his voice echoed across the great, dimly lit opening of the cave's entrance.

"Wait. I thought—"

"Good. You're using that space between your ears, Quinsey. I'm impressed," King teased. "One question. I trust you both read the booklet cover to cover. Inside and out. And memorized all of the techniques and methods. Am I right in assuming that?"

Their heads nodded like a dog watching a ball.

"Besides, I'm banking on your trust and comfort with one another inside a cave to be the real expertise here. My question is simply this: When something goes wrong, and it will, do you promise to have one another's back?" His eyes searched Quinn and then Cade. This was the BIG test? The one they'd lost sleep over all last night? This one thing?

*Unbelievable.*

"Yes? No? You plan to go home? What? Tell me if you can do this. And be straight," King said. "I want your word." He smacked the back of one hand onto his other open palm. "Right now!"

Cade extended his hand. "We always look out for one another." He shook King's calloused hand. Quinn did likewise.

"You boys aren't lying to me? Because I won't tolerate it. That far below ground, I might have to just leave you, if you don't resurface."

"No worries, King," Quinn said coolly, extending both hands palms up. "It's cool."

"And you have Cade, if he freaks out at the first sign of encroaching water?"

"He's done this hundreds of times, and—"

"With a *baby* cave," King countered.

Cade stepped in. "If Dad, I mean, Haven, can do it, then, I figure I can, too," he said, finding his voice, hoping to get a reaction from King.

"Haven sure would be proud. He sure would," King said quietly, not loud enough for either boy to hear.

Cade entered the cave behind Quinn, and he clicked the headlight to its medium setting.

"I recognize that light. It still looks to be in working order, too. You must've polished it or something," King said.

Cade shook his head no, not wanting to discuss the accident. "Just new batteries."

"It's seven o'clock right now. I expect to see you all, and your dad's gear, at 2:00 p.m. on the dot. That gives you six hours, and an extra one since it's your first go. Do you have the map? Tell me you do."

"Right here," Cade said, pulling a map out of his backpack. It was beside his map of Seton still. Then, King's words hit him fully and he stopped moving. "Wait. You're not going with—"

"Good. Use it as a reference. You might think I'm nuts for sending you out on this one alone, but I wouldn't do it if I didn't think you had *some* skill. Just don't die on me." He laughed awkwardly. "I need to know what you know."

"You don't know us," Quinn said bluntly. "Who sends rookies alone?"

King ignored the jab, and said, "See you after lunch. Go steady, and if things go bass ackwards remember: don't panic. Take care of one another. I'll see you on the other side. Then, I'll know you're worth your salt. Just be sure to tell me what you find." He gave a thumbs-up sign and walked away.

Just like that—the two were exploring the biggest cave in the world, on one of the hardest routes—and they were suddenly left all alone.

# CHAPTER NINETEEN

Quinn flicked his headlight off a few times for sport, and the reduction of light made it impossible to see. Cade stumbled over his own feet and couldn't find his hand waving in front of his face—just three inches away.

"You're a mouth breather," Quinn said.

"Such great company in a cave," Cade said. "Of all the people I could be sharing these walls with, it had to be *you*."

"One lucky dog, if you ask me." Quinn laughed, flicking his light back on. The intensity of the added light dilated both of their pupils. "Whoa Nelly!" Quinn said.

Their feet were just inches from a descent—a drop of at least eight feet. It would've turned an ankle or worse. Cade cranked his light up to its highest setting. "I don't want to take any chances," he said. "Not six miles in, or, six yards either, bro."

Cade pictured six hours of this, as he stepped into the abyss and found Quinn reaching out to grab him. The two would have to work together like never before. "You might want to crank your light down to conserve some juice. Man, we have a long day. The first level should be enough. I'll do the same," Cade said, aware of his breathing now, thanks to Quinn.

"No sir. I'm not breaking *my* leg. You can if you want. But then, you're behind me. So you can crank yours down and just follow mine, if you'd like," he said.

Cade agreed. This way if one light ran out, at least they could move his to the front and use its beam. "Onward soldier," he joked, clasping Quinn's shoulder. "Daylight is burning somewhere up there."

The two let his words echo around them, and it was evident that others weren't in Mammoth yet. The cave was a lonely monster. The pictures of Gorin's Dome from his spelunking guide still amazed him. Stephen Bishop, a slave in his youth, discovering all of these monumental things before tuberculosis got him. How did he do it? Cade wondered, looking behind them, as if he was on the trail, too.

"You talking to yourself again?"

"You know it," Cade said. "Seeing things, too."

"Don't push me into your delusions. I'm sure I wouldn't make it," Quinn said. There was another drop in the cave floor. He stopped and shone his light straight down. "Batter up?"

Cade jumped straight down without looking, realizing how stupid it was, and he landed with a hard jolt. His knees throbbed and he felt a splintery pain. Trying to act unharmed, he turned and thrust his hand up toward Quinn. The friend reached for Cade and let him absorb most of his body weight. It looked more fluid than it seemed, Cade was sure. But, who was watching anyway? Most creatures here had adapted to not needing eyes to look at rookie spelunkers; their eyesight was another source of fuel their body couldn't afford, so it left them over the years.

Cade rubbed his hands onto his jeans. "You need to let up on those Cinnabons," he said.

Quinn cleared his throat and walked in front of Cade again—leading the way. His light bobbed and weaved up and down the ever descending, ascending, one-story walls. Cade felt a thirst forming in the back of his throat, after what he imagined was at least two miles. It was hard to compare it to the cave at home. The one at the farm was mostly linear. Cade felt there were very defined A, B, and C points: the entrance, then half a mile later the dome, and finally a quarter mile later—the watering hole. Then, the wind tunnel had led them straight into a grass-covered thatch roof much like the one they'd found when they first discovered the cave. It was straightforward and impossible to get lost. Here, it felt different. There was risk. Every drop could be an injury and a full day's wait for help or longer.

Instinctively, he pulled his cell out of his pocket and admired how zero bars were penetrating through the earth's crust. Impossible for man to get to some places still. Just like the insides of Hawaiian volcanoes and craters on Mars. "Hey, shine your light up ahead," Cade directed.

"Yes sir, boss, sir," Quinn said. He shone his light where Cade meant, and it made both take a big collective swallow.

The size of their walking distance became a crawl—and fast, too. The crushing closeness of the trail triggered Cade's claustrophobia. He started breathing deeply, and the panic seemed to invade his psyche. He heard a voice, deep inside him say, *You're an Explorer*. The voice wasn't his, but one he hadn't heard in years, and it returned all at once. Cade looked at the hole where Quinn's light was directed. "Let's move."

They moved, but slower—much slower—than their pace the first two miles. Cade didn't have to worry about drop-offs or inclines now. His sole focus was on the dark tight space in front of him. Quinn's lamp light, blocked by the close quarters of rock, was rendered distorted and useless. Cade thought of progress as a distraction. It was the only thing he could embrace in the darkness. Had this been his dad's life every day as a welder? Tight and abandoned? The walls didn't let up, and for the next hour and a half he imagined, the two fought their way through knee and belly crawls. It was slow going, but the walls did recede, ever so slowly. Glee and oxygen invaded Cade's lungs. He stooped into a crouching position the moment he was able to give his knees a break. His back hurt like it did when he stooped to pick tomatoes at home. But, this awkwardness also passed, and eventually, the two were moving again with Quinn's light radiating fully ahead.

"Want to stop for lunch?" Quinn finally said, his stomach turning and growling around the walls.

"We can rest for a few," Cade answered. He retrieved his cell and noted it was already noon, and they still had a little over two miles to travel—neither knowing the obstacles. "Just fifteen. Then, we're back to it. King will be waiting at the pick-up spot."

"Will he?" Quinn plopped down and fished for the food prepared by the park staff. "He seems a little odd, don't you think? Like he never sleeps or something?"

Cade listened to the odd sounds that emanated from around them, maybe the walls themselves. Then, Quinn's stomach grumbled again. People a hundred years ago saw the same things. Maybe slightly different. The image of Dad climbing on this trail, mapping it with King, gave him goosebumps. Cade found his sandwich. It was roast beef, and the horseradish sauce was perfect.

***

When they stood, Cade felt the tension in his back. Stooping for hours made him feel old. Then, he recognized a *pitter patter* sound. The drips became more frequent. Quinn shone his light out a few dozen yards, and Cade saw his target. Water trickled and gained momentum from the walls and cascaded down, finding a river—the Echo. The one Bishop found while navigating this very same cave, according to Cade's book. Cade's fear of the water wasn't severe here; he knew Quinn was a strong swimmer, too.

The two paused for what felt like ten minutes and Cade noted the water's sound, still and serene, and perfectly timed. The drops resembled Christmas bells like the ones Salvation Army workers rang outside the Bigsby Market. The blind fish and shrimp appreciated it, Cade imagined. This never-ceasing lullaby kept their abyss at peace. Quinn gripped Cade's elbow firmly and pinched.

His gloved hand pointed up to the dome. The light from his headlight flickered, but revealed bats. *Everywhere.* The white nose syndrome was something King told them to be cautious about spreading; it was why they'd had to wear what he recommended the night prior, special boots and gear. This Wild Cave tour brought them into close contact with the nocturnal creatures. Thousands were resting, hovering upside down.

"Don't spook them," Quinn's deep voice said. "They'll drop all over us."

Cade remembered Quinn's comment to King about guano, and he caught notes of panicky fear in his friend's voice. He tried to stifle a laugh but couldn't. The sound echoed around the chamber. It's how he imagined an Egyptian pyramid, or, sarcophagus, sounding—utterly hollow.

"Shhh!" Quinn beckoned. But, there was movement above them. Squeaking and clacking noises started up. He clicked his light all the way off.

Pitch black darkness fell upon them.

Cade instinctively dropped into a ball and looked up to the dome-shaped ceiling. He couldn't see a thing but still pictured it as *mammoth*. The bats buzzed quieter than he expected, and the entire congregation never awoke simultaneously; it would've been deafening. Quinn made no movement to switch the light back on, and Cade pictured him holding his ears closed, facing toward the damp cave wall.

Then, as the squeaking squawks died away, he heard, "Cade? Hey fella."

"I-I'm here, Quinn," he heard his voice say in the darkness. "What is it?"

"Could you do me a solid and turn your light on. Mine was going out, and—"

"We're gonna need mine to get home," Cade flipped the light to the lowest setting, and he saw the fear (and tightness) of Quinn's freshly-shaven face. "Let's see how this trail finishes up," Cade said.

Quinn stepped aside and Cade moved to the front. He admitted the lead spot was nerve-wracking, despite the better visibility. Quinn followed too closely and a couple of times stepped on Cade's heel with his size fourteen shoes. "Guess I'm still thinking about those darn bats," he said, each time he bumped into Cade.

"No worries. I thought they were pretty wild. Guess this trail's name is fitting. Listen to that water." He held up his hand. Quinn stopped and both peered past the light's reflection onto more water. It not only sounded louder, but Cade saw more of it. Then, as if the trail would lead nowhere else, Cade saw that they'd have to hop over a portion of the trail where the water invaded. King warned them how the temperatures stayed the same (or relatively the same) throughout the year, but the water came and went in size much like it did above ground. There was flooding and drought, and there was erosion, in much the same way as the Grand Canyon. It all started with a river. The adventure was proving to be very real. Dad *Explored* this too, he thought.

"Watch where you're going," Cade said behind him. He stretched his body out above the dark, coffee black water, and he accidentally kicked a stone into the stillness. Hitting the water, it echoed loudly, and he froze.

"Don't leave me in suspense," Quinn's voice said. "I can't see anything, amigo."

"I'm trying to stretch across, but I don't think I can," Cade said.

"Those yoga classes with M didn't pay off then, did they?" Quinn tried to laugh, but his voice was hollow like a tomb.

"So, I'm thinking we're going to have to do something, and it might not be fun."

There was a pause and an exhale from Quinn's lungs. "I'm listening, Rainy."

"We're gonna have to run and jump over it, but . . . I think it's totally doable," his confidence waning as he said it. "Here, check it out," he added, letting Quinn peer over his backpack and around the two-foot-wide trail.

"You're funny."

"Got something else to solve this riddle?"

"Lead on, wise Sensei."

Cade didn't wait for more. He knew there wouldn't be anything else. Quinn's tell in a game of poker had always been his silence. He brooded when he was beat.

"All right. Tighten your backpack close to your body," Cade said, yanking his taut like a fishing line. "Then, just say when."

Quinn didn't speak. He only breathed deeper as an angry bull might—stuck in a loading gate. Cade said, "Here goes nothing." He loped in the direction of the murky Echo River. At the last possible second, he lifted his body as far upward and over the expanse as he could. *The weightlessness.* He landed and slightly stumbled—bumping his knee into the rock face. Before Cade could celebrate his leap of faith, he heard the *splash* and felt the cold water on his backside. Cade turned and saw Quinn clawing at the side of the bank. "Hold on, Bates!" he yelled.

"Just help me!" Quinn spewed between gulps of cave water. The cold droplets kept landing on his arms and chest as Quinn wrestled the Echo River.

"Grab my hand, and I'll pull you up," Cade tried to reassure. "Just grab it!"

Quinn swung and clasped Cade's hand on the first effort. He started to dip down into the chest high water again, but Cade put his muscle into the rescue and pulled his friend onto drier ground.

When he was aground, Quinn laughed and his teeth chattered all at once. "Geez, I didn't want to go swimming in there." He pointed. "I think the Loch Ness Monster lives in there. Thanks for saving me, buddy," he said, his solid physique shaking from the cold.

"Saved you from chest-high water," Cade said. "Some hero I am."

The two heard another sound and didn't recognize it. Were there bobcats and other things down there? Cade couldn't rule anything out, because this cave was so much more monumental than anything they'd ever seen. He imagined Mercedes' face lighting up with this tour. Could she do this one, without any assistance? He was sure she'd be up for it.

"Hey, Dora?" Quinn said. "How much farther do you think the tunnel runs?"

"Well, we could ignore the trail and follow this cave system for the full circumference . . . 400 miles, if you wanted to?"

"Punk."

"Just sayin'. I'm sure this light could make it another ten easy."

"Mine didn't even make it four miles. What makes you think yours would do another ten?" Quinn asked, always wanting to win an argument. "Did King know these would run out of juice?"

Cade didn't respond but let him brood. When he did see a noticeable upward slant, he knew the tunnel was taking them away from the Echo and to the exit they sought. He felt the burn in his quads and longed for a leveling in their altitude. How long would this steep grade in the trail go on? It couldn't do this the entire last mile, could it? But he was wrong. The final mile was grueling; there was no reprieve. It went up—straight up, to the heavens. Cade heard Quinn huff and puff behind him. The wet clothes were causing his teeth to constantly chatter. Cade wanted to pause, but didn't feel he could regain momentum, if he did. So, he hunkered when the trail went back to a small diameter, and the walls closed in. He pulled his elbows in and belly-crawled like a worm in a rainstorm. Cade put his head down, and even stopped looking at their progress altogether at one point. Quinn didn't object, because he was so close he followed Cade's hiking boots and was kicked again and again.

When the second light started to flicker, Cade thought it was an illusion—his eyes messing with him. But, they weren't. He flicked at the light with his thumb and index finger. It didn't help, and he started to panic. Quinn quickened his pace behind as well.

"Not much farther, I imagine," Cade said.

"Best just put the pedal down," Quinn agreed.

Neither spoke and the flickering light was interrupted ever so gradually by another raised, clear light. It didn't have a yellowish tint, and the light on Cade's head started to lose its necessity. Cade discovered that light was emanating from above their limestone cocoon. *It was the sun outside!*

"See it, Quinn?" his voice giddy.

"Keep moving. I don't want to die in this rock wall."

"We ain't going to die. This is it. We're here." Cade laughed.

He dug himself out of the hole with his remaining bits of energy, and he pulled Quinn from the tomb-like space as well. When they turned, both were lost in thought. Cade couldn't believe this awe-inspiring (and horrific) masterpiece rested just below the Kentucky surface. *Dad had been here before.* "We get to lead people through this," he said to Quinn, excitedly. "Can you believe it?"

Quinn grunted, and said, "I just need a shower. And, I'd like to get another shave before I see any of the girls," he said, stroking his face. "Think they'll be into me?"

"Girls that are here probably won't be seeing as much of you as they will the cave."

"They can have this one," Quinn said, pointing at the mouth of the trail they'd left. "Let's get up here, and see if we can find King."

Cade clicked his headlight off and loosened his backpack. He slung it off his shoulders and unzipped it. Inside, he retrieved a granola bar and offered one to Quinn. They munched ravenously on chocolate chips, oats, and molasses. When Cade took his wrapper and Quinn's and put them into the backpack, he saw King descending the stairway. He waved to them, and Cade shielded his eyes from the sun.

"Hello you two!" King said. "You survived Wild Cave, and I see you're almost unscathed. Almost." He pointed at Quinn's wet clothes, Cade's slight limp.

"It was that last jump," Quinn said. "It was something. A little warning might've helped us. Flashlights that lasted more than ten minutes, too. I—"

"The cave is different every time. You'll learn that. It's why a spelunker never fully masters a route. You must expect the unexpected. Tunnels collapse and rivers rise and fall. So, you have to work with the changes. Got it? It looks as if the water was up," he added, pointing to Quinn again.

"You don't have to look so happy about it."

"Don't mistake my smiling to be ridicule. I knew Cade's dad, Haven, and we went out all the time. I saw him slide into the Echo more than once. And, he never gave up. Ever. He was so ... *stubborn.*"

Cade's spirits rose as King relayed this nugget. "It's how I hurt my knee," he said suddenly. "On the last jump. I didn't keep my light up, and I lost where I was jumping. Ran my knee right into the wall," he said, smacking his forehead.

"At least you didn't leave Quinsey behind," Joshua said. "He's worth saving, I guess."

"So, how did we do on time?" Cade said, forgetting to check his cell.

"You all made it under seven hours. But, just barely. I was about to go down this steep end the wrong way, if you hadn't made the racket you did a second ago. I could've heard you a mile away." He fake laughed. "Glad you found your way. That's good for first-timers."

"Why'd you give us half dead lights to use?" Quinn asked again.

"What do you mean?"

"You said the bulbs were new, and mine went out, and Cade's almost did there at the end. Why? We don't appreciate being buried on our trial run."

Joshua looked the bigger, huskier teen over. "I wouldn't ever want to harm you guys. I think you learned a lot about each other, and the cave. Besides, you're too valuable," he added, looking at Cade, his eyes squinting.

Quinn *humphed,* but Cade was unnerved by King's words. *Valuable how?*

"That water was chest-high," Quinn added, puffing his chest out to King, showing him the water's level.

The three went back to the Visitor Center and dropped the gear off in the storage room. Then, they washed their hands, and Cade followed Quinn to scour for food in the cafeteria, looking over his shoulder more than once to watch King's path. Other spelunkers were huddled around a flat screen TV watching a documentary of Dr. Croghan's purchase of Mammoth Cave in 1839.

Quinn rubbed elbows with a few of the girls he recognized from WKU, trying to work his magic.

Joshua nodded to Cade and stepped outside of the center.

# CHAPTER TWENTY

Cade hopped onto the top bunk and flipped the nightlight on. He retrieved the journal, and opened to the third entry from Haven's pen. He leaned underneath the yellowish orange bulb and read:

*01 October 1982*

*King is a maniac! If there's one person that gives me a run for my money, it's that guy. Today, we hiked Wild Cave. He flipped his headlamp off and jumped down the 10-foot cave walls and didn't wait up. Wait . . . I take that back. He did stop long enough to wake the bats! Idiot. Thousands of them, and he woke them up. There was shouting and hollering, and the bats emptied their stomachs all over us. But, I'll not bore with THAT story. If you're reading this, it's because Hollie Johnston wants you to know how crazy I am. She's dying to go on the next tour. Can you believe that? Totally into any Adventure. Guess that makes three Explorers that'll still be here this fall, even though everyone else has left. Until next time . . .*

*Haven R.*

The familiar handwriting had plenty of smudges and shortcuts in its form. Cade appreciated how his dad wrote like he talked. Capitalizations and lost trains of thought. The cabin light was making his head hot, and he clicked it off. Joshua King was more familiar than he knew, or his dad told him. He wondered about their friendship. Had they had a falling out? Why hadn't Mom mentioned him before? As he closed the journal and re-snapped the band, Quinn entered, munching on a string cheese.

"These ain't half bad," he said.

"You're supposed to pull the cheese apart. It lasts longer," Cade advised.

"I don't need you telling me how to eat cheese," Quinn snapped, plopping into his bottom bunk.

"Those girls give you any numbers? Any glimmer of hope?"

Quinn let out a loud breath.

"You have all summer, don't you?" Cade added. "Plenty of *blind* cave fish," he joked, aware of his corniness.

"You're really fishin' for phrases, ain't you?" Quinn joined in, his laughter shaking the bed's frame.

The two talked about the girls in the Visitor Center. Quinn had met a tall brunette, and she'd introduced herself as Amelia. His voice rose an octave when talking about her spelunking confidence. "She just went on and on and told me she could outcave me. Can you believe it? She thinks she's better than me!"

"Wouldn't be the first, Bates. Look at M . . . she can spelunk circles around us," Cade said. Mercedes' green eyes flew into his mind. He missed their innocent, light-hearted quality.

"You know how to pick 'em," Quinn added, teasing Cade. "M is half jungle woman."

"She's exciting like—"

"Like you need to call her and stop telling me your every waking thought," Quinn joked, cutting him off.

Cade set the journal aside; he knew his friend was right. It was time to call Lexington. He moved his legs over the bedside and hopped down without use of the ladder. His legs throbbed from the day's beatings.

"Old man. Take it slow. No need to play Tarzan just because M is Queen of the Jungle."

"I'll knock that starry gaze off of you, buddy. Besides, I saw Amelia. Nothin' good will come from *that* brunette," Cade added, walking to the doorway.

He turned and saw the WKU baseball cap Quinn wore. It was college for Quinn and he seemed to be all in. The same thing was happening to M. Cade didn't have that and wanted it so badly. "See you in a sec," he said.

Quinn waved him away. "See you when I see you, pal."

Cade shut the door and went to the edge of their cabin's wall. He dialed a few digits and saw M pop up on the screen. Rather than dial the rest of her number, he just hit the call button underneath her name. It rang and rang, and went to voicemail. He didn't leave one, but instead sat down and watched the newcomers scurrying about like he had the day before. Mammoth Cave was already alive, and the extra bodies made it seem more life-like with every passing minute.

***

Joshua met him in the mess hall and asked Cade if he was busy. He said he wasn't; he was planning to read more of his dad's journal. Joshua leaned in and said, "There's something I think he'd want me to show you . . . if you want to check it out."

Cade said he did, still wary of his dad's friend. He put his dirty tray in the cleaning slot of the cafeteria and didn't even take time to brush his teeth; he was too anxious. What did King have in mind?

"My bike," Joshua said, pointing at a black Honda Shadow. "Get on."

"Good one." Cade laughed.

Joshua got onto the bike, and turned to look at Cade. "No joke. And don't worry about Quinn seeing you. He's in the café and very busy. I saw him talking to Amelia. He's not going to see you leave, believe me," he added, handing Cade an extra helmet. "Just a short ride from here."

Cade didn't worry about riding on the back of the bike as much as he did falling off. He hardly knew King. Grabbing the helmet, Cade hopped onto the back and snapped the chinstrap in place.

"You can hold on if you want, I don't care as long as you don't fall off," Joshua confided. Then, the bike lurched forward, and Cade instinctively latched onto the man.

The hot, suffocating humidity of central Kentucky receded as the bike picked up speed, and the cooler temperature triggered his memory of the chill in Wild Cave. Cade welcomed it, peering over King's shoulder periodically at the oncoming traffic, the twists and turns of the road.

They drove for what felt like ten, tense minutes, but Cade knew it was probably more like one or two. He waited for King to knock the kickstand down, and he slid off the bike first. Then, King turned it off, and removed his helmet. "Here we are," he said.

Cade took his helmet off, and the summer humidity stole the oxygen from his lungs again. It felt like a punch in the gut. Looking around, he wasn't sure where they were.

"This is it," he said, pointing down the hill from where they stood.

Cade looked and saw some water, boats moving into and out of a marina. "This is what?"

"I figured you and I could talk. How about it?" King asked, pulling fishing poles from his bike's saddle bags.

"How in the world can that hold fishing poles?"

"Collapsible, see? They work just fine. Just have to clean the fish intestines off before you put them back in the bin."

"Amazing," Cade said, aware of his high-pitched squeak. "Dad said you were crazy in his journal."

"You enjoying that? The journal? I figured you might. It's a good way to catch up on what he was doing out here," King said, indicating Mammoth and something else. It was the way he said it, Cade thought.

The two walked down the hill, and set up the rods, added the Zebo reels, and put bait onto the hooks. Once the lines were out in the water, Cade finally settled, said, "Thanks for Dad's book seriously. It's helped me. Plus, it keeps Quinn from bugging me to death."

"I think Quinn's distracted enough," King said. "And you're welcome. Haven *was* a best friend, like Quinn is to you. Do you like crappie or bass better?"

Cade thought about the quick shift in topic, and he looked out at the water. His heart sank a little, because his dad's last moments with him had been fishing at Spoonbill. The water didn't terrify him, but his memories did. He shrugged his shoulders, as he remembered his dad's love of catfish.

"Your dad always loved to fight a cat," King's lips moved, answering Cade's heart. "He fought those suckers pretty much anytime we weren't underground and he wasn't pestering Hollie." King laughed. "Those two fought like children. Well, you'll read all about it in that journal," he said.

Cade said, "Catfish . . . that's what I want to catch. You?"

"I'll eat anything we catch," King answered.

Cade re-baited the hook a bluegill had nibbled clean—its lips too small to take the bait under. Then, he recast the line with a jumbo-sized wad of night crawlers attached to it. He sat down beside King and watched the ripples move outward from where the baited ball hit the surface. The two waited and watched the Green River move with its own purpose.

# CHAPTER TWENTY-ONE

The fish didn't bite much.

Their bait became soggy. Then, an hour later luck turned and a few hooked themselves. With King catching three and Cade two, it was a solid enough effort for dinner. The two returned to camp somewhat victorious. They set King's grill away from the other visitors. Cade watched as King fileted the fish and got the pinkish, red meat from the spines of each one. He slathered melted butter and lemon pepper on each and set them over an open pit behind his cabin. The fire licked at the fish bellies. When butter dripped into the flames, the fire soared almost onto the fish—charring the meat slightly. King was quick to turn the fish at each char and never let the burn compromise dinner. Cade marveled at his efficiency. He must've done this a thousand times. The way he dabbed additional butter onto the catfish without burning his hand and flipping the fish effortlessly in the metal turning platter was something to see.

"Dang," Cade heard come from his own voice, deep and resonant.

"Dang what?"

"You're good at that."

"Tried and true methods take time," he said, patting more butter onto the fish, a lemon pepper coating now visible on each filet.

"It works."

King turned the fish a few more times and with a satisfied look said, "What do you think, Rainy?"

The way he used Cade's last name like Quinn did, he felt a closeness that wouldn't normally be possible so soon.

"Let's eat."

They plopped down on the smooth square stones, and each took a paper plate and loaded it down. King came back with two plastic forks, and after discovering this wouldn't really work, both started picking up the hot, smoky fish with their bare hands. The butter did help, Cade noticed. The lemon pepper, too. He was nervous, because he'd only heard of catfish being fried. In Seton, that's how it was cooked *properly*, Mom said. But, this tasted good, too.

"Nicely done!"

King clapped him on the back, and fish juice flew off of his fingers and into the fire—a loud sizzle erupting.

The two fell into laughter and munched on the grilled catfish as best they could, without burning the roofs of their mouths. "That fish is fighting back," King teased.

"I thought catching it was all we'd have to do."

"Down the hatch." King laughed, mimicking his best pirate voice.

They refilled their plates two more times, as their stomachs became bloated with Green River fare. Cade heard King mentioning something about Haven's affinity for three-pronged, treble hooks. The image of his dad casting again triggered an odd, eerie comfort. He leaned over onto another square stone and nodded off, as King continued his chatter about Haven's fishing prowess. It felt nice, he thought, drifting out like the ripples always did.

***

When he awoke, the grill was smoldering but the ashes were gone. He sat up too quickly. "Welcome back," he heard at his left shoulder.

"What? Did I doze long?"

"Just enough to snore and talk out of your head about school bus-sized catfish," King said. "But it was fun to listen to."

"Glad I could entertain," he said, less mad than somber by the memory of the fish story. "Something Quinn always said," he added.

"Haven told us the same things when we were kids," King said, off-handedly. "Always knew more than the rest of us somehow. Like God whispered these things in his ear at night."

"His journal reads like the way he talked."

"And you've read how many of Haven's entries now?"

Cade didn't respond, his voice caught in his throat. The pain in his stomach increased.

"We can talk about it, whenever you'd like," King said.

"Good. Because my stomach is killing me."

Cade heard a *crunch crunch* sound and saw Quinn walking over the twigs and branches, approaching their fish graveyard.

"What the heck did I miss?" he started. "Looks like World War III, and I didn't even get a text."

"King took me fishing," Cade said, happy he could boast about something Quinn could not.

"I see how it is, amigo. Leave Bill Dance at home and not tell him you stole his boat, huh?"

Quinn's fishing jokes were always lame, and Cade let this one pass. King didn't, and said, "I'm shocked you even know who Bill Dance is. He's before your time, Bates."

"We're on a last name basis now, too?" Quinn said. "I *did* miss out," his voice noticeably lower. Cade could always tell when Quinn was hurt.

"It's just a few catfish," Cade started. Then, added, "You can go next time. Right?"

"Anytime," their guide agreed. "Anytime you aren't leading amateur spelunkers into Wild Cave you can come out here and grill."

"Deal," Quinn said.

The three fell silent as they stared at the fish bones. Quinn finally interrupted, "King, can I steal Rainy for a bit?"

Joshua King waved him on. "You don't have to ask. We're all friends here."

"Let's take a walk. I gotta tell you something," Quinn said.

***

The boys walked along the trail, past the Visitor Center, but Cade's mind was still on the Green River—the fish fighting against his collapsible rod. He saw the catfish emerging from the water, fighting against his hook, the stuffy summer air.

"I talked to her," Quinn said abruptly. "Amelia. She's going to be a freshman at Western this fall," his voice giddy.

"The brunette?" Cade asked. "Or, *Trouble*. Isn't that what we'd labeled her?"

"Just a minute," Quinn pleaded. "She's better than you think and was the one who told me where you and King were. She invited us to breakfast tomorrow. She has friends, too." His eyebrows raised.

Cade shook his head. "Not a chance, buddy. You know I'm with M. She's my—"

"I know, I know. The only girl that really *gets* you. I've heard that for years. You want to at least meet these others? Bowling Green girls, man. They might surprise you."

"Fine," Cade said swiftly. "But, I'm not looking," he added accusingly.

Quinn folded his arms. "Why do you always have to be so black and white? Never any room for *what-ifs*. Maybe these ladies just want to talk? Amelia doesn't want to . . . but some of the others might. Who knows? Don't write 'em off, before you meet 'em. They could be cool. I want you to meet a few of 'em at least."

The two found their cabin and Cade retrieved his dad's journal again. He opened to:

> *11 November 1982*
>
> *It's cold outside, but the Wild Cave is constant year-round! No snow down there! Just the sweat and chill that comes from climbing. King can't keep up with me. I think about leaving him, but then, I can tell he appreciates it. It's not that he's a slower climber, he just seems to take in the sights longer than me. His first Expedition was all show with the headlight trick. I'm the Explorer Extraordinaire, and he's the Documenter. He likes to take a Mental Picture of everything, and I mean everything. Stop and Smell the*

*Roses to the nth degree! But, it's all right. We're here, and Hollie is showing us the cave shrimp, and the blind fish. I don't mind waiting, because it's letting me know where things are. I'm learning that everything goes somewhere. It's something I don't slow down enough for, but King does. He snaps a Mental Picture, an MP, and I wait. Hollie holds her own, but I know she likes the pauses, too. The Adventure is there, but we just take a little longer with it. I'm learning it's okay to take your time getting to the Adventures. It's okay to fight and acknowledge the Journey. I'm learning it's okay to be in the trenches. Here's to many more.*

*The park has officially shut down for the season, but we've been given the freedom to "unofficially" lead trips. Today's group was a group of World War II vets. It was really the best Adventure we've taken yet. King, Hollie, and I loved the group! We figured it wasn't the tour (because we took the easiest route with this group), or, the speed we spelunked, but the people. The older men were something special! Even though they were significantly older than us, these men were Fearless! They weren't just walking along and sight-seeing and oohing and ahhing over the rock formations. They WERE an Adventure! It was inside them. They didn't need the Wild Cave Tour. Frankly, they couldn't have done that tour if they wanted. But, their slow moving joints and arthritis didn't keep their spirits from hiking this cave. This was Mammoth Cave from an entirely different perspective. Imagine living life like that. Seeing it in them makes me want to live THAT Adventure. And, I intend to. If (big IF here) Hollie and I marry, I plan to be that kind of person. I'm on that quest. Living for that same reason these men were.*

*Haven R.*

Cade closed the journal. The writing still pounded inside his mind. He wanted to lean over the side of the bunk and tell Quinn.

But, when he stretched over, he saw the empty bunk. *That girl,* Cade thought. It wouldn't be long before the WKU girls were all flocking to Quinn, he imagined. He stepped outside the cabin and tried Mercedes' cell again.

After three rings, he heard her voice come to him in a rush, "Cade, I'm so so sorry . . . I meant to call you back. This camp is insane," her sweet voice complained, but didn't sound unpleasant. Not to him. He held the touchscreen close and didn't move it from his ear—afraid of losing his one bar of service.

"Cade, you still there?"

"I am. Just listening to you," he said. "You sound so good, even when you're tired. You know that? I've missed that voice. Does that sound desperate or what?"

"I don't think so. Desperate is reaching for something that isn't there. I'm here. Or, well, you know what I mean. Here, in Lex, but I miss you like crazy."

"How is Lex? Is UK as awesome as you imagined?"

"Monstrous," she laughed. "But not like the caves. It's a beautiful campus, but I miss the caves. And you and Quinn and your lover's quarrels," she teased.

"Call it what you want. We're still bickering just like always. He's found a few Bowling Green *people* for us to meet at breakfast tomorrow," he added.

"He always does. And, I'm sure he wants you to hang out. Be his wing man. His steady?"

"You know us better than we do ourselves, babe."

"Well, I don't have to pry, but you know I wish I was there to knock them away," her voice distant, just a little worried. "It seems Quinn never knows when to latch onto one that's good for him, does he?"

"I'll keep him from getting into places he doesn't need to be," Cade reassured.

Mercedes exhaled. "You know I love you. I'm not sure why I picked riding horses over spelunking with you boys."

"You did the right thing. You love riding horses, training them."

"I *love* being with you," she said, and her voice sounded strained. "Equine science will be here anytime."

Cade knew she was fighting back tears, and he just wanted to soothe her. "I'm in Bowling Green. I can come visit, if you want. Luckily, Lexington isn't on the moon."

She laughed a little bit. "I know. But, don't worry about that. Just think of me and remember the cave at home . . . our first kiss. I think about it every day. It's *our* spot."

Her laughter was infectious. His spirit rose, and he thought of his dad's journal again. He blurted, "Dad left me something!"

Mercedes' end of the line went quiet. "Cade?" she said, her voice distant. Then, there was static. "Cade? What did you say? Something about your dad? Is there any news?"

"M, you're fading out. I can't hear you—"

"Cade, I'll call—"

"I'll tell you later. Ok—"

"Love you, Cade."

Cade's phone *blipped* shut. The cell tower failed. He stared at the abrupt end to the phone call. It said the duration was four minutes and twenty-nine seconds. That brevity would have to be enough for now. He put the cell phone back inside his pocket and rolled over on the bunk. He stared at the cinder block wall and it felt reminiscent of the prisons he'd seen on TV shows. He tried to close his eyes, but the restlessness continued. His overly full stomach, Quinn's obsession with girls, and Mercedes' distance felt insurmountable. The summer suddenly felt like a weight on his shoulders, and he didn't know if he could carry it.

# CHAPTER TWENTY-TWO

Cade fought the hand away from his leg.

"Get up!" he heard, coming through gritted teeth. "Today we get to teach the newbies about Wild Cave and guess who's coming along? Amelia!" Quinn beamed, too impatient for Cade's answer. "We gotta move!"

"Do you hear yourself? You sound like the Tooth Fairy came and delivered a dollar under your bed. Calm down! I thought you were Mr. Cool when it came to the ladies," Cade scolded, his stomach doing backflips.

"You don't look too hot," Quinn said, peering at Cade's pale face, sweaty and unwashed.

Cade held onto his stomach as he shifted in the bed. "Ughhh," he muttered, acknowledging the bad taste in his mouth. "Lemon pepper didn't sit so well." He lunged off the top bunk and knocked into the trash can.

As unkind noises came from Cade, Quinn watched with mouth agape. "Man, c'mon," he whined. "The one time I *want* to be out there."

Cade fought the battle with freshwater fish and lost. He held his head over the trash can and waited for it to end. Quinn came to his side and held out a wet washcloth.

"Thanks, man. See, I knew you cared about your buddy," Cade strained. "Maybe we can go caving after all," he said, his face disappearing just as quickly inside the can again.

"Rainy, I wouldn't ask you to do that, even if you were my enemy. And, you're a trooper for even offering. Amelia . . . well, she can wait," he said resignedly. "The cave has been here for millions of years. What's a few more hours?"

"Thanks, bud. I don't think I could make it to the door to be honest." Cade stifled a painful laugh. "Catfish didn't go—"

"I'll go get King. Let him know. And, I'll try to get you another bucket," Quinn said, disappearing out the cabin doorway.

Cade clung to the can and made sure all was at bay, before pushing himself to where his back rested against the hard wall. He held the washcloth to his forehead and closed his eyes. The room spun ever so slightly, giving him a sense of vertigo. The image of a Bayliner and his family swimming at Cumberland invaded his thoughts. His stomach quivered and he was back at the can. He wrestled and felt he was losing again and again. Eventually, he heard footsteps and glanced over the metal rim to see Quinn leading King into the cabin.

"Boy, I didn't think catfish could fight so, but you did eat about three yourself, didn't you? That's my fault," he consoled. "I should've stopped you."

"It tasted so good," Cade said. "A man should know his own limits, and I didn't."

King and Quinn grinned at his attempt at humor. Neither spoke, as King pried the bucket from Cade's fingers. The teen relinquished his hold slowly.

Then, King produced another metal tin and pointed at it like a mime. He grinned, and his rough-hewn, bearded face looked odd smiling.

"You puke there," Quinn spoke for him with a caveman tone, stifling his laugh with a fist in his mouth. "Sorry, man."

Cade knew he looked silly, but his stomach was empty at least. He waved them away. "I'll be fine. Go on. My day'll come."

"We aren't going without you," King said.

"Yeah," Quinn added, trying to sound less defeated than he was. "You're the ring-leader, amigo!"

Cade looked up to his top bunk, mumbled, "My journal," meaning his dad's. "Could you grab it?"

King did, and Cade rubbed the washcloth across his forehead.

King opened and eyed the journal. "You gotta stay healthy, because you're my mainstay for Wild Cave this summer. Without you, there'll be a lot of unhappy cavers," he smiled.

Cade dabbed at his splotchy face.

"I need you more than you know," King whispered barely above a whisper.

"And Quinn *has* to see Amelia," Cade added.

"Cade, man! I told you in confidence. C'mon!"

Cade took the outstretched journal, flipped it open.

"Cade? Cade, there's something else I wanted to tell you."

Quinn looked at King, and Cade waited for him to continue.

"Your dad and I were best friends like we talked about yesterday," he said.

"I know. He wrote about it. Wild Cave, Gorin's Dome, and the Bottomless Pit. Amazing!" he said, excitement causing his stomach to heave again.

"Watch it," Quinn urged. "You'll be right back where you were."

"I agree," King said. "Maybe we can wait 'til later to talk."

"Where am I gonna go?" Cade asked. "Go ahead and say your piece," he said, holding the journal close to his sternum.

King cleared his throat. He rocked back and forth, and it wasn't a gesture the two boys had seen before. He looked nervous about something.

"Your dad and I *were* close. Almost like brothers. You and Quinn understand that." He looked and neither spoke. "We came here for adventure and found it. In more ways than one like—"

"Hiking with the vets!" Cade said, excitedly. "I read that one last night. Spelunking in November." His stomach jumped again, and he slowly inhaled.

"I knew I should've cooked the fish longer."

"I'll be fine. It's not your fault."

"Well, what I was going to tell you can wait—"

"Just tell me," Cade said.

"Yeah, out with it," Quinn said, over King's shoulder. "Now you've got us both interested."

"Haven and I caved and explored for months, but this place had one more adventure. It really tested us. We—"

Amelia suddenly bust into the cabin, winded. "Joshua. We have a situation in the center. Two girls are fighting over the gear. I tried to break it up, but they wouldn't listen. It's getting ugly! Sorry to interrupt . . ." her eyes darting to Cade on the floor, Quinn with his tanned face, his crimson chin pointing straight at her. She fidgeted, "Please, Joshua. They're pulling hair."

"We'll talk later." King turned to go.

Quinn followed Amelia out of the cabin.

Cade wondered, not for the first time, why his mom or dad, for that matter, had never mentioned Joshua King. The chaos of girls and boys chanting, "Fight! Fight! Fight!" penetrated the cabin walls.

Cade didn't have a clue what King meant, and a curveball felt like it was coming right at him. He flipped the journal open and devoured more of the entries—the Bottomless Pit in all of its glory, Gorin's Dome and Dad's reference to Stephen Bishop more than once. He relished the descriptions, but he started to note a slight distancing—a disconnectedness between Dad and King. His dad made less references to their escapades. Cade took a deep breath. He saw the conflict reach its pinnacle, when his dad specifically mentioned King not belaying for him at a two-man pass. Then, Cade read that King unhooked the ropes attaching the two and threatened to turn back and leave his dad where he was—the bottom of a pit, insurmountable. Cade shook his head and considered closing the journal. His stomach was empty and so was he. Where was this going? Maybe it's what King started to tell him? He read the next entry's date:

*20 December 1982*

And, he thumbed to the following page, and saw a monstrous jump in time to – *1995!*

He flipped back a page, read:

*20 December 1982*

*King has lost his marbles. He threatened to leave me staring up at Gorin's Dome! Can you believe that? Me, his best friend! Just staring like a turkey in a rainstorm about to drown, because I'm too stupid to know what he's doing. He's gone mad, but I know it's more than that. He's trying to make a move on Hollie. It's obvious. It took some time, but now I see it. The Bottomless Pit and Wild Cave are just two examples, but I've known since the vets came that he's gone off the deep end. The way he looks at her. I catch his gaze every so often. He's as guilty as can be. I wouldn't be so mad, if I knew he didn't stand a chance. He's better looking, and . . . Hollie does talk with him on the side. I've seen them at the main entrance staring into the abyss some evenings. And, they ain't talking about bats. King's really trying himself. Today, was what it took to wake me up. My head has been too far into Adventure. So, I'm going to make it simple for both of them. <u>I'm leaving.</u> Plain and simple. No drama from this Explorer! Tomorrow, I've arranged to* *take the bus back home to Seton. It's where I belong. I'll spend time on Cumberland. Maybe get a job coal mining. That sounds good! Hollie will be able to make a decision, and I'll be at a safe distance. I don't want to be belayed to my death, and it's not that I think he'd do that under any "normal" circumstance, but Hollie isn't an ordinary gal, and we found something* ***else*** *that might be clouding his brain, too. Something that might make anyone go too far. What else can I do? That's it. Seton, here I come. Hollie, if you get this darlin', know that I want you, but I also want to LIVE. Greed isn't worth it. Come find me. God willing, I'll see you two and a half hours east of here. Give my love to the Green River.*

*Haven R.*

The end of the entry struck Cade to his sickened core, and the journal plopped to the floor with a thud. How could he? His insides waged war against him, and he searched for Joshua King through the cabin's window. *He was supposed to be Dad's best friend!* Cade's anger didn't last long, as he felt exhaustion overtake him, and in a few seconds he was on the floor—spilled over like a can of open Pringles.

# CHAPTER TWENTY-THREE

The cabin floor creaked as King approached Cade on the wooden planks. The young man was startled awake and pushed himself from the cabin floor too quickly. In doing so, he felt a splinter jam into one of his palms.

"Easy does it, Rainy," King soothed. The journal was splayed on the floor beside his shoe.

"I read all about it," Cade said, holding his palm close to his side. "How could you, you backstabber?! I thought you were Dad's friend. Was it all a plan to take Mom?"

"Let's just calm down. Bring it down a few notches."

"Why? You deserve it. Leaving Dad down in the Bottomless Pit."

"No, no. Don't be foolish," King said, a little too harshly.

Cade recoiled from the man. "Leave!"

"I *need* to say this. To clear the air. Okay. I was never able to with Haven."

"He left," Cade answered. "He left, because you became insane and tried to steal Mom."

"But, did I?"

"You tried."

"I did. But, I wasn't successful . . . and did you notice anything else?"

"Thank God."

"Read the letter again."

"Dad won."

"He did," King consented. "He got Hollie, and she went to Seton, and I stayed right *here*." he pointed to the wooden planks. "I was blinded by the beauty—"

"Don't talk about Mom."

"Read his letter again. I didn't see the cave anymore. And, I was blinded by what they had. It wasn't my business. Even if Hollie wanted to talk to me."

"Shut up!" Cade shouted, echoing around the cabin's space.

"This is what I've wanted to ask for thirty years. Since Haven left . . ." King trailed off. "Did you get anything else from the journal?" he pried. "Anything at all?"

Cade didn't respond. His chest heaved in and out. What was his angle?

"I wanted to apologize to him. But, I can't see. I can't. I didn't get to. I prayed for a chance, and I asked God to forgive me for picking my desires over my friend. He was *my* friend. Then, I heard about you through Quinn. And, when he said your last name and where you were coming from, I put it together. And, I was excited. About how I'd tell you. How this would go down. And, I didn't want this," he said, pointing between himself and Cade. "I didn't want the yelling and shouting. I put my friend's life on the line. I was choosing the girl over my friend. It would be like Quinsey leaving you, and I wouldn't wish that. But, I did it to Haven. And, then, I read about Spoonbill, and I was so sad to hear of his passing."

"You don't know anything," Cade said coldly. "And, why do you keep looking at me like that? What did Dad mean by you getting greedy?"

"Let me have a look at that splinter. Looks deep."

Cade looked out the window. He saw a fiery red cardinal perched on a tree branch. It hopped from limb to limb excitedly.

"I want some time alone that's what I want, King. And, I'd appreciate it if you knocked, before you barged in here," Cade said, matter-of-factly. "For privacy."

"I'll never get a chance to ask Haven's forgiveness, but, I can you. I'm asking you."

Cade watched the bird *hop* along and dance from branch to branch. Then, he saw a brownish red companion, and he knew the one was trying to woo the other.

***

Quinn returned, wiping his hands on his pant legs. He boasted a Band Aid over his eyebrow. Quinn's hand went up in a *Wait a Minute* fashion. Cade looked at him and did just that. The stifling heat billowed in under the door. It searched its way into the room and brought perspiration to both of their foreheads. Cade wiped his away. "Well?" he urged, when he could stand it no longer.

Quinn pointed at his eyebrow. "See this?"

"Love wound?"

"I wish," he said. "It was one of those younger girls . . . high school no doubt, but I got to break up the fight, and Amelia was there."

"Yeah. So?"

"Amelia was there and we brushed elbows in the scuffle. She got in there and helped me pull the smaller one away from the WKU student, Kate, I think. In the midst of it, the scrapper clawed at mid-air, as I pulled her away, and she caught me with a nail," he said proudly.

"Let me get this straight," Cade said, leaning up on the bunk bed. "You got a cut from a high school girl, and you're proud of it?"

"See, it wasn't like that. I—"

"I can put it together, I believe. And nowhere in the recreation does it have you coming out a hero, man," Cade said, forgetting for a moment his fight with King.

"Not fair. I did it for Amelia," he pleaded. "I wanted her to be wowed by my strength. The way I handle things."

"I think you did a fine job," Cade egged on. "She's certain of your powers now," he said, pointing to the Band Aid. "But, I wouldn't think you've won her over. Imagine if she meets a guy who stands his ground and claws back at the next high school girl? Then, she's got a real decision on her hands." Cade held his ribcage, his empty stomach—laughing so hard.

Quinn smacked the cabin wall too hard, popping his wrist. "Ouch! You're bad luck, Rainy. You know that? If I keep hanging around you, I might lose a limb before long," he said, rubbing his wrist. After a few moments, he reached for Cade's hand, said, "I heard you picked up an injury earlier, too, can I have a look at it?"

Cade recoiled, cradling his throbbing hand.

"Chill, 'kay? Let me see."

Cade flashed his palm outward from the bunk bed, and Quinn gave it a once over. "Looks like infection will start in soon."

Cade couldn't argue. He saw the swelling had doubled from earlier. "Do you think we should amputate?"

"Seriously. I can have it out in no time. And I won't charge what the other guys are charging."

Cade admitted the thought of letting King look at it after their scuffle was less than appetizing. He muttered, "Do you really think you could get this one out?" he said, showing a three-inch, wooden dagger hidden beneath the surface of his right hand—redness encircling the splinter already.

Quinn nodded, as perspiration fell from his forehead. "Been wanting to use my Gerber on something ever since Christmas," he said. "You're the perfect specimen. Let's begin, and you'll be a new man in no time."

With those words, Quinn extracted his shiny, hardly-used serrated knife and flicked his lighter on and held the flame under one side of the blade. When it seemed to satisfy him, the teen flipped it over and heated the other side as well.

"Just making sure there's not any fish guts or anything to impede our surgery," Quinn said, flipping his handsome grin to Cade.

"That knife looks so new I doubt it's ever left the sheath," Cade gulped, his joke falling flat—his nerves showing through in the way his uninjured hand gripped the comforter.

"Plenty. Plenty. Now, let's get this over with," Quinn said, approaching the mattress with the blade locked into position.

"You're sure you know what you're doing? I mean, I'm not going to have to give up being a cave guide before we start."

"Trust me like you did in Wild Cave," Quinn said, clamping down on Cade's knee.

The recent memory of the trail gave Cade's heart a flutter, a palpitation. "Just go steady with the blade. If it's as sharp as it looks it might do the job without you needing to pry much."

"Don't worry. Do you need Benadryl or something to take the edge off?"

"I'll be fine. Just go in at the top of my hand closer to my fingers. You know, where the splinter stopped? And work it back toward the edge of my palm. It shouldn't take much force . . . or cutting," he added squeamishly. Then, he took a gulp of air—his mouth completely dry.

"My word. No cutting unless necessary. Hey, maybe it would help if I told you about my plans for wooing Amelia?"

"I'm good. Besides, I know you'll tell me when I'm below ground and don't have anywhere to run. Could you just get the thing out and I can hear about Amelia's God-given beauty later?"

"Deal," Quinn said, already gripping Cade's right wrist with his left hand, prying with the side of his knife blade down—forcing it out.

Cade withdrew and forced Quinn's grip away. He instinctively held the wrist in his left hand and looked at the red swollenness, the festering wound which throbbed like a heartbeat.

"Man up, Rainy. This has to come out, or, you won't make it through a week in the caves."

Cade held his hand and stared down at it and waited for Quinn to take it back by force, but his friend waited patiently. Finally, he opened his mouth, but he didn't say what Cade thought he would. "You and King gonna be all right? Or, am I going to have to go find a new bunk mate?"

Cade looked down at the Gerber in Quinn's hand, and rather than talk more about his dad's old friend, he welcomed the blade. "Bring the knife. Cut me, Mick," Cade said, a long-standing reference between the two from Rocky—their favorite film.

Quinn said, "Well played, champ," and he took Cade's hand, held it gentler than Cade thought possible. "I'm going to turn the blade sideways again and press down—"

"Are we going to talk about it, or do this thing!"

"—until the foreign object is free of the body," Quinn finished, his best physician voice at hand.

"Just do it, Bates, and I'll listen to anything you, or Amelia, ever want to say to me."

Cade felt a searing pain burst from his open palm, as a metal blade met the surface of his skin. It pushed and pried until the object dislodged and was forced part-way out of his hand. At that moment, Quinn closed the knife. "Would you like to do the honors or shall I?"

Disoriented and afraid to look down, Cade said, "Just get it over with!"

Quinn expertly dropped the knife into his pants pocket, and with steady hands, plucked the large splinter free from Cade's palm. "Sit tight. I'll go get some Neosporin and whatever else I can find. Be back before you can shed a tear," he said, springing for the door.

When he returned, he saw Cade propped against the wall, and he dabbed the Neosporin onto a large, gauze-filled bandage and fastened it to Cade's hand.

"You're pretty good with that knife."

"I like you, too. Even though you don't want to hear about my new girlfriend. She's not *that* bad, I promise."

"She's no M."

The two rested and Cade turned the bandaged hand over and over again.

"At this rate, we'll have some epic war stories for when we get back home. If we go back to Seton," Quinn surmised.

The image of his dad's letter flooded his mind. He'd found something else with King in those caves, and King was willing to kill him for it. But what?

# CHAPTER TWENTY-FOUR

Cade saw sunlight cascading through the window and onto his bed.

He pushed the comforter back from his legs, and as he did, he saw his hand. The bandage was almost unnecessary—the Neosporin working its magic overnight. He hopped off the edge of the bunk and he shook the cabin's frame when he landed.

"Whoa!" Quinn said. "Sasquatch lives."

"This stuff really works," he said. It was still tender, but he didn't want to grimace in front of Quinn. Besides, it wasn't as bad as some of the blisters he got from digging. He remembered Abbott requesting him to dig non-stop.

"I need to look at it."

"You're not Mom, are you?" Cade asked, pulling his hand back. "Let's go caving," he said, grabbing his gear and getting outside, away from the stuffy quarters.

"Man, wait up!"

Quinn swiped his brown hair out of his face—trying to keep up.

"King didn't think you'd be ready." He gasped. "At least for a couple of days. What with your food poisoning and now *this*," he said. "He wanted you to take it slow. I can go with him, and he said he could work doubles on Wild Cave Tour. You don't have to go until you're ready. He said that . . . not me."

"I'm sure he said a lot of things," Cade said over his shoulder.

Cade pushed into the Visitor Center and went straight past the other cavers and Mammoth tourists. At the back, he grabbed his headlight, helmet, and boots King required them wear. Then, when he saw Quinn alongside him, he said, "Better move fast, if you want to keep up with me today."

"Will you dial it back? Amelia and her group are supposed to go with us. Whether it's you helping me, or King, and if you don't slow down, it's gonna be King," he said, face in a frown. "I need you, man."

Cade's hands shook as he laced up his boots, and Quinn went to the lunch table. He came back with a couple of peanut butter sandwiches and a carton of 2% milk. "Drink up, bro. You won't make it a mile if you don't!"

Cade nodded and devoured the protein, carbs, and Vitamin D in record time. Then, he gave the remnants—empty plastic bags, paper carton—back to his friend.

Quinn took the trash and found a receptacle outside the room.

"You're my best friend. I want you with me on these tours, and I don't care if you date the entire troop of girls at Mammoth. You know that?"

"I told you to slow it down. You're not making any sense, and I'm afraid you did more than just eat bad fish."

"No, I meant the journal," Cade said, pointing back toward their cabin. "Dad's journal. He wrote about King and Mom. King had the hots for Mom just like Dad did. Except Dad left Mammoth in '82, and the two didn't speak again."

Quinn stared blankly at Cade, eyes unblinking.

"I meant to tell you last night, but I've been a little bit *disjointed,*" Cade added, bending his wrist and pressing on his recovering hand.

The door opened at the Visitor Center's rear entrance, and King entered. His eyes flickered from Quinn to Cade.

"I'll see you down at the main entrance," Cade remarked to Quinn, ignoring King as best he could.

"Listen—" King started to say.

"I don't think anything will be as refreshing as a six-mile hike through Wild Cave. Do you?" Cade asked Quinn.

Quinn light-stepped from one foot to the other, nervous at his friend's behavior. "I think we should wait a minute. The rest of the group should be—"

"They'll catch up, if they want to cave with us today."

"You boys are under my leadership!" King demanded, his experience showing through, and something else. "In case you find anything, I'll be right here."

Cade flinched, but he kept his eyes on Quinn. "Let's go, amigo. The cave is waiting."

Quinn looked at King for any other order, but none came. He glanced at Cade's resolute, scruffy jaw, his bloodshot eyes. "Okay. Lead on, Rainy," he said half-heartedly.

"I'll go with you boys, if—"

"Nope. We'll be just fine. We've spelunked before. Besides, I believe you've already led plenty of other expeditions, haven't you? Even peoples' moms have been on Wild Cave with you, haven't they?"

King waved them away, and Cade was already marching toward the cave's entrance. Quinn spotted Amelia and two other girls en route to the main entrance, and he flagged them down, yelling, "You can go with us, if you hurry. Two *experienced* cavers right here."

Amelia beckoned her two friends from Western to catch up to the racing boys. All five went into the cave and embarked on Wild Cave. Quinn lagged behind intentionally, making sure all of the girls were prepared—checking their gear, joking with them about packing their lunches properly. Cade put his helmet down and clicked his headlight on, imagining his approach to be identical to his dad's in '82, before the world turned upside down on Haven Rainy for good.

***

The girls were silent as the party advanced inside Wild Cave. Mammoth was darker, more sinister than Cade recalled from a few days prior. His restlessness led them forward. Who did King think he was? What did he want? Quinn tried to tap him on the back, but Cade wouldn't relent. They scaled walls and descended them like they had in their first trial, but it didn't feel right. Something was off.

"If we could just slacken the pace a little, it would give them a chance to catch their breath," Quinn offered. "Then, we could pick up—"

"Do I need to wait for them at every turn? Couldn't I just go on ahead and you could deal?" Cade said, his face flushed. "I don't see why they came!"

Amelia shielded her two friends, Leslie and Keisha, from his rage—echoing around the cave walls. "It's okay. We're fine," she soothed.

Quinn's chiseled, normally calm face looked incredulous with lips even and eyebrows furrowed in Cade's headlight. "Not cool, Rainy. These girls are why *we're* here! The reason we came here this summer. Would you just let your anger go for a minute? We need you down here. For our safety and theirs." He pointed to the girls behind him.

"We can turn around and go back, if y'all want to go it alone," Amelia said, pretty face resolved to turn back.

But Cade knew it was pointless. The cave was too difficult to turn around and exit like the one in Seton. Wild Cave was too finicky; the walls too narrow and the circumstances too unpredictable. Plus, he *wanted* to press on. His anger was his catalyst for *Exploration,* even if he couldn't enjoy himself—distracted by King. He simply shook his head at Amelia, her company.

"We better follow the maniac," Quinn tried to tease. Leslie and Keisha were hesitant to move, even with Amelia leading them by their elbows.

"Come with me," Cade said over his shoulder. The four followed him deeper into the limestone fortress.

Above them Cade spotted bats, some with white noses and some without, and almost all were stirring from the noise. *Just rest your eyes and sleep you miserable creatures! We'll be out of your maze soon enough,* he thought.

Cade felt a second tap on his back, as he heard the *clomp clomp* of Quinn's boots on the cave floor. "What?!"

"Are you going to let up on the gas, or, am I going to have to lead these gals alone for the next four hours? Since you're dead set on completing it in record time. Because . . . I don't know if they can."

Quinn never admitted defeat in anything. Rather than offer consolation, Cade heard what he didn't want to say rise to his lips, "I didn't tell you to bring them, bro."

"It's why we're here at Mammoth. Why else do you think we'd be working as spelunkers all summer?"

"Adventure."

"It doesn't pay, man. We *need* to work to save up for this fall," Quinn pleaded. "That's why I'm here. And them," he said, pointing behind him. Amelia nodded, as if on cue.

"I don't need to," Cade said, even though he knew he needed work. But, he knew he didn't have college. This only made it worse. He said, "College brats," and stormed off again. His insides churned with the peanut butter sandwiches, and he stalked through the cave, knowing the walls would tighten ahead. Why was he being like this? Dad was gone. It wasn't their fault. Not even King's. His pace had the girls gasping, and Quinn working triply hard to help them with their novice skills.

They loomed farther back and Cade only scanned behind him twice—from the bat domicile—to where the cave walls shrank—to the suffocating belly crawl he'd remembered earlier. It felt like ages since he'd been down here, instead of only hours. His claustrophobia at the fissure cave returned and he gasped for air. Not wanting Quinn and the girls to see, he instinctively fell to his knees and prepared to start the tight crawl. The apprehension and fear built inside him, and his churning stomach met the trepidation head-on. The peanut butter sandwiches knocked against his stomach, and he answered with a dry heave. In a matter of seconds, his only real meal in two days was gone. The girls turned their heads, and Quinn reached down to his friend's helmet and helped him turn the light off. Even in my lowest moment, he's there, Cade thought. What a friend. *And I've been a jerk all day!* He wiped his mouth clean with his gloves. "Thanks, man." He flipped the light back on, and it penetrated past the girls and into the dark trail behind them. "I'm sorry about my—"

"Attitude problem," Amelia answered.

"Yeah. It was uncalled for."

"No worries. We figured you heard something really awful to make you so mad. Did your girl break up with you or what?"

"No. It's not that!" Cade said, angry that Amelia jumped to that conclusion. "It's something else. Let it go. Normally we have to conserve batteries, but with the pace, I figure we're ahead of schedule." He grinned at Quinn. "My friend wants you all to learn as much as you can while we're down here. He's usually right, and I'm sorry for being such a jerk. Losing my lunch seems to have cleared my head." He tried to laugh, bile still agitating his esophagus.

"Quinsey told us you two were the best. Can you help us master Wild Cave?" she flirted.

Not wanting Quinn to lose face, especially with a girl that called him by his full name, Cade said as coolly as he knew how, "You already are."

***

Quinn made sure his light remained off and told the girls behind him to do likewise. The space was so tight that having a headlight on was just pointless—wasting batteries. He went on to encourage them to not freak out if their feet, legs, limbs were hooked in a crevice. It wouldn't do any good to jerk or wriggle around. Somebody would just get hurt. "Ball up as best you can and treat the cave tunnel like you're a nightcrawler and you're on a path. The only difference is there are a lot of other worms traveling with you, and if you stay close to the one in front of you, you won't fall behind or cause the others to either."

Cade started laughing and muffled his mouth with a glove. It was either the most unique or absurd comparison he'd ever heard, but it was Quinn. He was full of surprises. When Cade crept on to the eventual opening, he stood up slowly and felt the emptiness inside his gut. Quinn stood beside him and fished in his pack, when he turned, he offered a protein bar. It was carrot cake. Cade's favorite. Cade finished the entire bar in three swift bites. Then, he crumpled the wrapper and stuffed it into Quinn's pack.

"You're welcome."

"Water?"

"Back there, too," he said, pointing to his backpack.

"What would I do without you?" Cade teased, gulping down mouthfuls of cold liquid.

"Get a new best friend to mooch off of."

The girls snickered behind him, and both boys turned to see them rifling inside their packs as well. Amelia handed more peanut butter sandwiches to Leslie and Keisha. The girls were hard to see inside the cave, but upon closer inspection, inside this larger chamber with the Echo River reflecting in his headlight, Cade saw their features a bit better. Leslie and Keisha were completely different in looks. Leslie, blonde-haired, blue-eyed, had skinny, boyish features to her, and she looked fragile to the touch. But, Keisha's fiery red hair, tanned face, and curviness countered her friend. Cade looked away and felt his face redden. It was odd to worry over embarrassment inside a cave, but he did. Amelia was a mutual blending of the two, Cade surmised. The headlight shone onto her athletic form; she possessed both sandy reddish hair in pig tails and an even tan. Quinn caught Cade looking with his light, and elbowed him. "Easy, *friend*!" he said. "Do you have a death wish?"

Amelia, Leslie, and Keisha were all obviously aware of his gawking, because they laughed at Quinn's comment. Is it a gift girls have to always know when they're being noticed? He rubbed his stomach. Content to have the protein bar, Cade yawned.

"Listen, those girls were just telling me how cute they thought you were. I didn't mean anything by what I said. You know that."

"Tell them I don't need to be told I'm cute. I know that already," Cade said snarkily. "Besides, I'm with M."

"Of course. How could I forget? You only say her name like a million times every day."

"Good. Glad I made my point. She's the one," Cade said, trying to not look back at Keisha anymore.

The Echo River was slowly moving past their feet, and his dad's words struck him. He heard, *You're an Explorer just like me!* The words empowered Cade. He didn't have fears of cave critters, fissures, or even the slow moving water at his feet. *Maybe I could swim in it like Abbott showed me?* He found himself pulling his shoes and socks off, and he was sticking his toes into the frigid water. It wasn't more than forty degrees. But still, he waded out and felt the chill consume his ankles, his calves and on up his knees and thighs. At this point, Quinn was rushing to the water's edge.

"You can't even swim that well!" he urged. "Let's get a move on to the rest of Wild Cave. Okay? These girls are pretty exhausted. We don't need to add hypothermia to the list of problems, do we?"

Cade looked up at his friend on the dry limestone edge and laughed. "I thought you were the *wild* one?"

"You know I am," Quinn said, crossing his arms, trying to act tough. "It's just . . . it's just that I told King I'd have them back before dinner. We need to be there, when the cafeteria ladies have sloppy joes ready." He tried to laugh but fell flat. Quinn's voice was constricted, and the tension didn't sit well with him. "C'mon. Get back here, before I have to go in and get you."

"I'm not even waist deep." Cade laughed, feeling freer than he had in ages. The cave's darkness and blind wildlife everywhere *was* an Adventure, he admitted. This is it! He laughed and the echo traveled back out the nightcrawler-sized space. "I think I'm in love with Mammoth." He laughed, and the bats chirped a good distance away in response. "See, the bats are too." Cade splashed a little and the term 'spelunking' took on a new meaning. It was more than a hike on limestone. It was a swim through pitch black darkness.

Cade felt Quinn's large palm on his shoulder, and Quinn tried to pull his friend from the abyss in one swoop. The hand startled Cade, and he lunged out into the middle of the cave. Quinn toppled into the black, wintery temperatures of the cave water. Cade's headlight, and his arms flailed out above him—going up and down out of the water.

"Just hold on!" Quinn bellowed, spewing water from his mouth. "I told you to get out!"

Quinn reached again and again for Cade. The cave floor dropped off significantly, and the depth of the water was well above Cade's head. He fought the liquid and lurched forward and back—his head remaining below. When he did manage to claw his way back up, he gasped for air and took in a big gulp of the wake he'd stirred. Then, he went under again, and the girls said, "Save him! Do it now!"

Quinn dove into the spot where Cade went under, and he smashed into Cade's flailing torso like a linebacker. When he had him, Cade spun around in the water, so cold that it felt hot, trying to ricochet his way back to the edge. The girls jumped away, but then, Amelia rushed back and extended her hand. Quinn's meaty paw enveloped her hand, gripping her wrist as he yelled, "Help me pull him in!"

Keisha grasped Amelia's waist for added support. Leslie reluctantly did the same to Keisha. When Quinn pulled Cade up to them with his other arm, he said, "Pull!" The three helped, and in a minute Cade was back on the rocky bank, motionless.

"Does anyone know CPR?" Quinn asked, and suddenly Keisha lunged down, doing chest compressions, counting aloud, and trying to revive Cade.

"Cade? Cade?" she said more than once to his supine frame. "Stay with us."

"Have you done this before?" Amelia asked, worried.

"Lifeguard every summer ... more than once sadly," she confirmed. Then, her lips went back to Cade's, her hand went over his nose as she blew into his mouth. This went on for several seconds, and Quinn paced back and forth. Leslie didn't know what else to do, so she clasped her hands and prayed.

"Just save him!" Quinn yelled at Keisha.

"Shouting doesn't help," she said evenly. "He will or he won't," she added matter-of-factly.

The finality in her voice sent Quinn into a bigger rage, and he kicked his own backpack and sent it flying across the trail. "No!"

Then, with a *whack* across his sternum, Keisha was able to get Cade sputtering and spitting water, regurgitating it everywhere. He coughed for a solid minute or two, and Quinn was at his side.

Cade saw his friend bumbling in front of his blurred vision. "Wh—what—did I do?" he asked.

"We're here, partner," Quinn reassured, hugging his friend. "You almost left us on the Echo River. You would've left if Kesha--"

"It's Keisha," the redhead corrected. "And, you were the one who jumped in after him," she said. "I just did CPR."

"CPR? You did CPR on me? And, it worked?" Cade said.

"You're breathing, aren't you?" Keisha beamed.

Amelia patted her friend on the shoulder. "My girls. See, Quinsey. I told you they would prove themselves worthy. Hmm?"

Quinn nodded, "You're right. *We're* sorry for doubting. Won't happen again."

Cade was helped to his feet by Keisha, and she told him to walk around a bit and see if his disorientation let up any. She kept saying, "Take it slow. Slow and steady. Don't rush. We're not in a rush. Our lights are still working. So, if your light burns out . . . we'll still have two more," she confided.

"When did you take over?" he asked, doubting her sudden tone and change in demeanor. Was this the same girl who barely spoke before?

"I didn't take over. But, I did get a little more say when you went under water and came out blue and motionless."

"Okay." Cade held up his hands. "I'm thankful to be alive. And, 'thank you,' for bringing me back. But, now I'm *here*. I'd like to take back over, if that's all right with you. There's still a good bit to go past Echo River."

The two made eye contact, and their combative back-and-forth dialogue was friendly, Cade realized. He was thankful she wasn't trying to act hateful, as he had earlier. He regretted showing that side of himself. Quinn had picked solid rookies for this first trip.

"I'm sorry for almost dying back there, everyone," he said.

"Don't try it again," Keisha said.

Quinn said, "You gotta get back to M, pal," clapping him on the back, putting his hiking pack around his shoulders.

The mention of his girlfriend's name sent a spark through his mind. She would've never known how he'd died, apart from what Quinn said. He shuddered at the thought, especially since his dad disappeared the same way.

"Let's move," Cade said, his voice echoing around the sarcophagus-like tomb.

Cade's headlight revealed small, creepy eyes all around Wild Cave. He caught Keisha looking at him. He turned toward the exit. "To daylight," he said, as he led them to the final crawl space and eventually to the world above.

# CHAPTER TWENTY-FIVE

When they reached the surface, King was there. He received Amelia with outstretched arms, as Quinn scratched his head. Cade felt the sunshine penetrate his damp clothing.

"So, what's happening here?" Quinn asked.

The two let go, and Amelia turned to him. "My uncle. He's been here since forever, and I told him I'd visit this summer. Don't worry, you're not on a hidden camera somewhere," she teased. "Although, if you were, your look would be priceless," she added. "Quinsey, close your mouth."

Cade made eye contact with King, and he saw the conniving look resurface. Before he could speak, he heard, "I'm sorry for saying it the way I did. For not telling you first thing. The journal wasn't the best way to handle our *history*, but I thought you'd like to know your dad's side first."

"*His* side," Cade started, anger rising inside him. "What's that-"

"Wrong wording again," King laughed. "I'm 0-for-2. Help me out, Amelia."

"It's your story, Uncle Josh, not mine. Besides, he's still here, isn't he?"

And he was. Cade stood in place—exhausted, wet—waiting for more. Why? he thought.

"Your dad can tell you things I never could. Not in the way he could. The bond you had. He was your dad. But, I knew him, too. I wanted what was best for him."

"Except for Mom," Cade said.

"The heart wanted what it wanted," he said. "But, I'm glad Haven left the caves and went to Seton. You know that? Because when he did Hollie went after him. She didn't wait a minute after reading that journal. She was in Seton that same night." The look on King's face was hopeful, held together by a thin-lipped grin. "Your dad won her fair and square."

Cade noted King's squinting, red eyes. He looked at Amelia, and she didn't do or say anything. Then, he saw King offer his strong, calloused hand.

"Wanna shake on it? I promise I never pursued Hollie after that. Her and Haven were together. I was here at Mammoth."

"Whatever you say," his lips uttered, but his heart relaxed—its pace slackening somewhat. "What were you doing exactly?"

"Caving like a somnambulant," he smiled. "I was a sleepwalker."

"Joshua's a good guy. He's why I came this summer," Amelia interrupted, standing closer to her uncle.

"Hey!" Quinn interrupted. "I thought *I* was the reason you came. To learn how to spelunk with a *real* caver."

"You know what I mean!" Amelia countered, her two friends snickering behind her. "Joshua is the most experienced guide in Kentucky, and he's worked in the biggest caves in the world for thirty years. He—"

"Why are you soaking wet?" King redirected. "Your clothes are drenched."

"You shoulda seen him down at Echo," Quinn started.

"Quinsey, stop it!" Amelia hushed. "Cade, he . . . he—"

"Went for a swim." Keisha stepped out, around her friends.

"Yeah," Amelia corrected. "What Keisha said. He shocked us and dove into the water."

"Is that the truth?" King asked Cade. "Did he jump in?" He turned to Quinn. "Last I recall, he couldn't swim well. Why would he just take it upon himself to dive into something that could kill him?"

Quinn looked to Cade. The two stood still for a moment.

"Cade has an adventurous spirit, just like his daddy, I guess," Quinn remarked. "I just can't seem to peg him sometimes."

Cade winked slyly, and King didn't seem to notice. He stared at Quinn with all his energy. When King looked to Amelia, he said,

"You girls better keep an eye on Cade, we can't have him *disappearing* on us," and his voice sent a shiver down Cade's spine. "He's why we're here."

The way he said it. It didn't sit right. Why would he disappear? Why was he their reason for being at Mammoth? It didn't add up. Then, he realized it was tied to his dad somehow. "I can take care of myself," Cade said tight-lipped. "I'm not a baby."

"No, you're not. You're almost a grown man. And, I want to keep it that way—"

"I'm going to my cabin," Cade said, walking past the group, his helmet on, light still beaming.

"Cade. Wait up!" Quinn said.

The two turned to go, and Amelia side-hugged King again. She said, "It's been a tough day."

"You girls all good?"

"Never better," Keisha said, staring after Cade and his friend.

"Don't worry too much. Cade's right where he needs to be," Joshua said.

"I hope you're right," Amelia said.

***

Mercedes called and said she'd be there by nightfall. At camp. And when she arrived, Cade knew he'd be beside himself. He already was; his palms were sweaty and his legs tapped uncontrollably over the side of the bunk bed.

His mind raced over the afternoon. *I almost drowned. I swam in the darkness. Some girl named Keisha gave me CPR.* It was Keisha's lips he'd felt. *She saved me.*

What did King want? Cade knew it wasn't just the cave keeping him there for thirty years, or guilt. He felt the journal under his pillow and took it out. Cade tried to read more of his dad's entries after he left Mammoth, but it was too disjointed from the present. He turned the journal upside down and shook it. Every page was intact.

Then, he gripped the pages and tried to see if any were different somehow. Nope. What am I doing? What was King after? He was about to toss the journal at the wall, when he saw his dad's inscription of the single word *Adventure* etched on the final page glued to the back panel with a slight arrow drawn upwards. Something King had never tampered with or anyone else.

He shifted on the bunk, causing the entire frame to shake.

"You wanna talk about it?" he heard below.

"Hmm?" he responded, not thinking about Quinn at all, forgetting he was there.

"You know you can talk, if you want."

"M will be here soon . . . at Mammoth. I told her about the swim and she freaked. She wouldn't listen," Cade mouthed absentmindedly, trying to keep his friend at bay.

"Well, you want to see her, don't you?"

Cade pried the glued journal page away from the back cover with his fingers, and a thin, sliver of paper fell onto the bed. He scooped it up and held it to the ceiling light – some sort of map?

"Well, do you?"

"Do what?!"

"Want to see her?"

"Why wouldn't I? She's my girlfriend. Wouldn't it be crazy not to?" he added, searching his insides. He arrived at Keisha again. It was crazy, but he couldn't move past it. She'd saved his life, and he didn't know how to think otherwise.

"Keisha is—"

"Keisha's what?!" Cade said, startling even himself. "She didn't pull me from the black water you did! You're the reason I get to say 'Hello' to M."

"You and I know that's not all. Keisha *saved* you. She resuscitated you. CPR wasn't my move, man. My hands were tied. She stepped up."

"So what? Even if she hadn't, I would've been fine. In a better place. Heaven," he said, angrily. "Anyways, I gotta show you something."

"Do you hear yourself?" Quinn countered. "You would've been dead with M none the wiser. Now, you get to see her again. You gotta give Keisha *some* credit. What's with you?"

"Nothing! Just that she you know? She kinda kissed—"

"Whoa, buddy."

"Shut up!" Cade scolded. "I need to tell you something else. Shut up about Keisha for a sec, will ya?" Then, he paused for some reason. *Can I tell him? Will it just put more people in King's way?* The map was some sort of serious find, if his dad hid it from everyone else all those years ago. Like he knew it wouldn't be found.

"Keisha is your Wendy Peffercorn," Quinn kidded.

"I don't watch your old movies," Cade demanded.

"Sandlot. C'mon. You know it. Squints fakes drowning to kiss Wendy. Remember that scene?"

Cade was too focused on his dad's map. He jumped down from the top bunk and heard himself ask, "What would you do?" Unsure of why he even asked it.

"About Keisha?"

"Never mind. I just need to go for a walk."

"No, No. Just hold on a sec. I know what you're sayin' . . . if I know one thing, it's women," Quinn confided. "You're in love with M, of course. She's our best friend. Seton gave us a perfect snow globe. And today, with you almost dying, you're looking at Keisha and thinking, 'Who's this chick? She saved my life.' And now you're like, 'I don't know anything.' Right?"

Cade admitted it didn't sound quite so stupid, coming from Quinn's mouth.

"And, now M's coming *here*. To Mammoth. And, the world suddenly is a lot bigger. M is *it*, but Keisha throws a wrench in the whole thing. Am I right?"

Cade thought it over. *Bingo.* Mercedes was his world. But who the heck was messin' with things?

"Why're you looking at me like that?" Quinn folded his arms, leaning against the bunk bed post.

"Her lips were what I felt when I came to. It felt . . . *good*," he admitted. "Like I knew I shouldn't enjoy it, but I *did*. The water didn't snatch me like it did Dad. And, now I'm alive but I feel dead somehow. Do you get that?"

Quinn looked at him for a long, silent minute.

"You know M better than I know any girl," he said, countering Cade's long-held belief. "She's your girl. You know that, don't you?"

Cade agreed, and he hoped his friend would have his back when it mattered.

"And, she's going to be there for you," he said, smacking Cade hard on the shoulder.

"Jeez' man!"

"Let's get you ready for the ball, Cinderella," Quinn said, ending their deep discussion. "You'll show M all we've learned in our brief time here. Don't freak over what happened earlier—"

"Why would I tell her about Ke—"

"I meant the drowning. Not her," Quinn said firmly. "You didn't kiss her. You were resuscitated. Got it?"

Cade felt his head bob up and down, but he wasn't so sure. His time spent waiting for his cell phone to vibrate felt surreal. *I'm on Mars, and it's just me and the Rover and red sand. I can't handle this isolation.* But, the cell did vibrate, and stole his mind from King and the mystery map. He looked at the incoming name and saw *M's* picture on the screen. She was going to be there for him. Just like Quinn said. He hit 'Answer'.

"Cade Rainy, talk to me!"

And her voice was the sweetest, most concerned voice in the world. Not motherly the way Hollie's sounded, when they'd first learned of Dad's disappearance. Not even understanding the way Quinn's did, deep and resonant. It was *affectionate* and . . . a part of him somehow. It was an embrace across the distance she now traveled.

"Be there in fifteen. I'm on I-65. Love you."

He said likewise and meant it. But, as he hung up, he felt a nagging uncertainty return, and he didn't like it one bit.

# CHAPTER TWENTY-SIX

The bonfire was blazing, and Mercedes' headlights crept to the flames.

The trio of Amelia, Leslie and Keisha were on blankets listening to another caver, Mike Trestle, strum his guitar. He picked his acoustic to a Cage the Elephant tune, and M accidentally stepped on one of the girls' blankets.

"Excuse me," Leslie said, seeing the stranger hover above them.

"Oh, I'm sorry. Hey—"

"You're—" Leslie said.

"Mercedes McCall . . . from Seton," she tacked on.

"Oh. That's right! Quinsey said you were coming," Amelia said. "You're Cade's girlfriend, aren't you?"

The question caused Mercedes to step back from the blanket, the girls. She said, "Yes? . . . Cade didn't tell you I was coming?"

"He's been in his cabin all afternoon," Keisha said, dejectedly. Then added, "It's nice to meet you. Is your name spelled like the car?"

"Where's his cabin?"

Keisha's look remained downcast, her frown prominent even in the flames from the fire. She pointed to the lone cabin at the end of the path leading from the Visitor Center.

"He's still alive, isn't he?" she asked the girls. "You look like you've seen a ghost."

Keisha just shrugged. "If we hadn't been there, he might've not made it."

"You're the one who saved him?" she said. "I'm so sorry for being rude! Thank you! Thank you for that!" she said, walking toward the cabin.

Keisha looked after her, and said to neither girl particularly, "Why can't *I* talk to him?"

"She's the girlfriend," Leslie said, without adding anything else.

"Can you play something else?" Keisha asked Mike Trestle.

"Like what?" Mike said, pausing mid-strum in his best rendition of "Cigarette Daydreams."

"Just nothing slow. Please?"

"I've got one," he said, as he strummed quickly to a new tune.

***

At the cabin, M knocked twice and Quinn opened.

"He's in here," he said, solemnly.

"It feels like a funeral around here."

Cade saw her brown locks and green eyes. There were slight rings under them, and he could tell she was tired. But, she looked as beautiful as ever. He tried to remember the last time they'd kissed. It'd been at graduation. Her smile, her lips, had met him there. He'd embraced her and squeezed her in a hug—harder than any ever before. Tonight, he hopped down from the bunk bed and wrapped her up in an even bigger embrace than that. His injured hand stroked her cheek. He said, "Are you all right? In Lex, I mean?"

She kissed his hand. "Cade Rainy, you know I'm okay. It's *you* I drove here for and you want to know about me." Her laugh escaped her.

Quinn laughed, too. His smile appeared, and he looked to be happy spirits were rising. "What took you so long, M?"

"The pedal was all the way down," she retorted. "I don't drive a Lamborghini."

Cade leaned in, kissed her gently on the cheek. Something he didn't usually do. It was almost always the lips, he thought. Then he whispered, "M. You're here now. That's what matters."

She didn't react with the cheek kiss, but she did weaken at his words.

"Tomorrow's a new day," Quinn said, chugging a bottle of Yoo Hoo. The moisture from the bottle dripped onto the wooden floor.

"You hoodlums better be glad I came when I did. I don't know if you'd have survived another day. Some *Explorers* y'all are," she teased. "Am I right? Cade being resuscitated by what's her name?"

"Keisha," Cade said a little too quickly.

"It was terrible," Quinn said, coming to his friend's aid. "For *all* of us. But, we got him back, and we don't plan to lose him again."

Mercedes' beautiful, doe-like eyes searched Cade's—looking for something he couldn't place. He looked away and took a swig of his semi-cold Yoo Hoo. The chocolate, milk-like beverage flowed down his throat. He said, "It'll be just like old times. We'll be spelunking like we always did, except—"

"This is *Mammoth*!" M said, grabbing Cade's T-shirt.

"Epic!" Quinn chimed in. "You have to see those chambers in Wild Cave. They kick the Seton cave into the ground."

"Don't knock *our* spot, Quinsey Bates!"

"Yeah," Cade said, coming to her defense. "That place *is* special. No one else in the world knows about it. Except Mom and Abbott, of course. And maybe one day—"

"We can get back there and treat it like this," M said. "Maybe offer tours to the Seton kids. Wouldn't that be sweet? Our good deed."

"Exactly what I was thinking!" Cade said. And it was. He suddenly wanted to be back in the Appalachian foothills, and it was something he never thought would cross his mind. "It's our thing. When we go back, we open our cave to the public. Agreed?"

"Some public," Quinn snapped. "Seton?"

"Agree to it!"

"Fine! When we get back, we're going to turn your mom's land into a tourist trap. Fine by me," Quinn said.

"Good. The sign going into town will read: *Welcome to Seton! Population 581. Home of Cumberland Lake & Haven's Cave.* Sound good?"

Mercedes and Quinn looked at their friend like he'd lost his mind. But, they agreed. Cade set the Yoo Hoo bottle down. He kissed M until Quinn cleared his throat. The three laughed, and it felt like old times. Cade said, "Wanna go for a walk?"

She said she did.

"I won't wait up," Quinn said, and went in search of Amelia.

Cade took his girl's soft, tanned hand into his and walked past the Visitor Center. It was pitch black except for the lightning bugs, and for a moment he forgot about Mammoth Cave below their feet, his father's journal resting in the cabin, and the secret map tucked inside his pocket. This evening reminded him of home, and he was okay with that.

# CHAPTER TWENTY-SEVEN

Joshua King introduced his niece, Amelia, to Mercedes, even though the girls met the night before. (The girls had slept awkwardly in the same cabin.) He gave strict instructions to the other guides to take a *personal day*—explore the other sites within Mammoth at their own leisure. He looked Cade fully in the eyes and made sure his intentions were known. Then, he gathered gear and placed it all at the feet of his two protégés—Cade and Quinn. King found headlights, helmets, ropes, and tools Cade didn't even know existed. He instructed Amelia to get two sandwiches for each caver, two granola bars, two apples, and two bottles of water and have them all wrapped up and placed in brown paper bags, set aside for their backpacks. He was explicit that they were to be prepared this time. No more mishaps.

"You're too good to have these setbacks," he said, driven by forces unseen. "Cade knows what adventure is and he better conquer it before it—"

"Joshua?" Amelia asked. "Uncle Josh?"

King didn't pause at her words but kept dropping supplies in front of them.

"Josh!" she said firmly. "If they don't want to go, you shouldn't force them."

"They wanted the *full experience*. Isn't that right gentlemen?"

Neither moved, nor spoke.

"Quinsey looks beat. Why don't we all rest for the tourists coming tomorrow?" she said.

"Nonsense," he responded, over the mound of gear. "This is what people do in Kentucky. They ride horses, and they cave. And we came here to cave. Mercedes left horses in Lexington to be *here*. It seems we're all on the same page. *Almost*. Let's do it."

A few murmurs came from the girls. M looked to Cade and caught him looking dejectedly at the ground. It was a look he didn't wear often. Then, he looked across the mound to Keisha. He hadn't seen her in the daylight, he realized. It'd only been inside the dimly lit cave. And, now, in broad daylight he discovered she was even more exquisite. Her eyes were exotic and green, like Mercedes'.

M saw Cade's gaze go right past her to the girl from yesterday. She cleared her throat. "Mr. King. I think caving *will* clear the air. I can't wait to get down there. It'll be like old times," she added. "Right, you two?"

Cade cleared his head. He looked at his girl's eyes and saw green pools. He almost paused to compare hers to Keisha's again but thought better of it. "I'm not afraid of anything, M."

"Dang skippy," Quinn added. "You know I'm not afraid of Wild Cave. Third times the charm," he bragged, looking at Amelia.

"I feel like we're pressing our luck," Amelia said. "Besides, we can't just leave the other guides alone . . . to roam around the park."

"They're not alone," King said. "If they have *any* hiccups they know what to do on any of the other assisted tours today. Plus, I left instructions with Doris."

"So what's the plan?" Cade said, tired of King talking. He looked from M to King and crossed his arms. *He wants what Dad found, at any cost.* "We cave or we talk about caving. What's it gonna be?"

Amelia threw up her hands. "Fine, fine. Y'all win. But, if something goes haywire, remember this 'I told you so' moment."

Mercedes sized up Keisha and looked back to Cade. "I told them I'd get back to Lex *after* I made sure you were okay. If this is what you want, I'm gonna go with you."

"If it means that much, then come right along. There's plenty of room, but . . . it does get tight. It's harder than the Seton cave," he warned.

"Bring it on," she said, rolling up her sleeves.

Keisha tugged on Leslie's shoulder and whispered something. Amelia said, "Grab one piece of gear each, girls. This day just got interesting."

King printed duplicate copies of the cave map, even though Wild Cave was one he'd explored thousands of times. *Does he know I found Dad's map last night? Is that why he's acting odder by the minute?*

"All set?" Quinn asked.

Cade scooped up his gear, fastened his rope to the backpack, and said to Quinn, "Just like old times, huh?"

The two stalked off at a quicker pace than the rest, and M struggled under the weight of her gear, but she caught them by the time they'd reached the mouth of the main entrance. The trio of girls and King brought up the rear. Mammoth awaited them a third time.

***

Cade took the lead and M found him. The two walked side by side, while the cave permitted. She reached for his hand a couple of times, but never quite held it like they usually did—fingers interlocking. He shone his light into her beautiful eyes and saw the backs of her irises. She held up her hand and blocked the glare.

"You look even better under a magnifying glass. You know that?" he flirted, trying to not think about his dad's map in his pocket—the thing marked with the letter X.

She playfully smacked him on the behind, and he slowed his pace.

Quinn, watching from behind, said, "Hand check, kids," with his deep voice booming around the hollow cave rim.

Amelia slid up to Quinn's side. She whispered, "Let them have their fun, if they want, Quinsey. They've earned it." He backed away, and Amelia did as well.

"Did you miss me, Cade? Really? Did you, or, are you just saying it?" Her eyes searched his, as they walked at a slower speed, under dripping limestone walls.

"You know I did. Hey, did you know there're horseback trails at Mammoth?" Cade said. "You could stay here and ride."

"I will, if you will. I don't want to do anything you don't want to do. I'm here for you. Remember?"

"I know. You're the best. Have I said that yet?"

"You better start saying it more."

He felt an urge to look behind them—to see if Keisha was within listening distance. But, he didn't.

King's voice said, "Cade, let's slow our pace to a crawl, when we get to the first wall climbs. Okay? Some of the girls will need a little boost."

"Got it," Quinn answered for him.

"I heard," Cade muttered.

"You need to let up on Joshua," M said. "You said it yourself that he admits he was wrong, and he just wants your forgiveness—especially since he can't have Haven's. Not now."

"I know what he can't do. I was there when Dad *disappeared,"* he said, air leaving his lungs. *If you all . . . any of you only knew who he really was.*

Cade reached out and climbed the first ten-foot wall without any help. Then, he turned and reached over for Mercedes' hand. She gave it, and he hoisted her over.

"Shouldn't we help Quinn and—"

"He's a big boy," Cade interrupted, looking straight ahead at the other obstacles in the trail. "He can pull his own weight . . . and all the others' I'm sure. And, if he falls, he has King to pick up the slack. King's the king," he sarcastically mouthed and snuck a peek at his dad's map with his headlamp. *Getting closer.*

M waited for Cade's light to shine back into her face, her eyes. When he turned and it did, he saw the horror in her countenance. She looked baffled by his words. "Do you really mean that? You can't. He's your best friend."

Cade didn't know what to say. He let his actions speak, as he offered his hand at each shift along the walls. He hoisted her, carried her over the thresholds, like a new husband would a bride, but his heart raced. He stole a glance behind them and saw Leslie helping Keisha over a dip, King closely following.

"Forward progress is *this* way," M said, softly into his ear, making him shiver. Her purr and the damp atmosphere gave him a chill that went straight to his core.

"Cade, how's it looking up there?" King's voice echoed. "See anything *unusual*? Anything worth mentioning?" he pried.

"Treacherous as always," he said, forcing himself to speak to the veteran guide with reluctance, obvious disdain.

"It evens out soon," he promised, and it did, into Gorin's Dome and the bat enclave, where thousands of wings greeted him like old friends. "Let's keep our voices down," Cade mimicked, his voice lowering significantly.

"Yeah. We don't want guano landing on our heads," Quinn said, voice shaky. "Let's keep it clean."

Cade paused. Then, he said, "Would one of y'all like to lead?" His mind was a thousand miles away.

Mercedes said, "We're doing fine. Treat it like *our* cave. It'll keep us from freaking out. That's what I'm trying to picture . . . even though Mammoth is scary big."

Her lower lip quivered. Cade held her by the shoulders. "I won't let some white-nosed bat get you."

She relaxed slightly at his attention. The rest of the group slowed with Cade. King rested his hand firmly on the young man's shoulder. Neither spoke, even though Cade wanted to break the man's fingers. The bats above were quite restless, and it was the most movement Cade had seen in their three trips.

When Quinn unexpectedly sneezed, the bats awoke and guano fell from Gorin's Dome en masse; the squawks were deafening. Cade spun around and saw Amelia covering her ears, and Keisha and Leslie covering their heads. He tried to duck, but it came anyway. King stood stock still beside him.

"Gross!" Quinn blurted.

Cade shook his head, even though he wasn't looking.

"Those bats only know one thing and it's this: lights shouldn't come back here and they don't belong. So, they wake up startled . . . and freak out!" King shouted.

Quinn said, "Wouldn't they get used to these tours?"

"Maybe if we came in here and stayed for longer stretches," King said. "But, we're only here for a few minutes. We're the misfits. Wouldn't you freak out if a bat tried to live in your cabin with you?"

Quinn sneezed again. They hunkered, waiting for the bats to disperse into a deeper recess of Wild Cave. Cade noted it was the same direction they were headed, and he felt a connection with the bats. Much like them, he was disturbed by the interruptions and intrusions. The squawks and shrieks kept him moving forward. Mercedes and the rest followed, as he led them to where he almost died the day before.

# CHAPTER TWENTY-EIGHT

The levels of the Echo River were higher, and the currents swooped into and out of the cave system where they walked. Cade high-stepped the water as it lapped at his ankles. He tried to caution M, but she pushed his hand away. When he turned to her beautiful face, she looked elsewhere.

The others waited for him to move forward with her in tow. Finally, they paused in their belly crawls and the cave opened up. At the edge of Echo, Mercedes said, "I need a sec," and she waited for him to respond. Maybe argue otherwise? But he didn't; he felt tugged to leave her alone. And, he just gave a slow nod, his helmet bobbing up and down.

"I'll be over here with Quinn," he said, looking in the direction of Keisha. His heart was racing. Why in the world would he want to look at her with his girl here? He couldn't answer his own question, his palms clammy and lips drier than ever.

"Whatever. I'll have a peanut butter sandwich by *myself*," she muttered.

And the sudden change in her stunned Cade. He'd never seen M react that way. She was never the jealous type. Her quick, scolding eye made him nervous, but he backed away in the direction of Quinn—flirting with Amelia.

***

Mercedes looked out at the water and fished a peanut butter sandwich from her pack. She propped herself on a smooth, flat rock and let the pack fall to the ground with a *clunk*. No one noticed, and then, King came over to her side. He said something Cade couldn't quite hear, but he knew she was now in conniving hands. *King had moved in on Mom . . . why not my girlfriend?*

Cade said, "Quinn, what's happenin'?" His voice rose with the tension in his throat, but he tried to not break eye contact with his friend. Then, he did steal a glance at Keisha and saw her nudging him with her head to a bend in the cave, just away from the opening where everyone now rested.

"Cade, I'm busy. Can't you *see* that?" Quinn asked, incredulously. "Give a guy some room," he said, referring to Amelia.

"Fine by me," he said and held his hands up again. *I'll just play the victim here*. "I'm not wanted," he said under his breath. Then, he turned and followed Keisha's light around the corner. He figured M saw it, but he suddenly didn't care. This girl *did* want him. So, he followed.

When he rounded the corner, it was pitch black where her headlamp shone a second before, and he started to shout for her. But, a soft, perfumed hand came up and covered his dry, chapped lips. She said, "Shhh," and her voice was even, her breath melted and chocolate sweet. "Just relax. I've been thinking about you ever since—"

"Ever since I almost died?" Cade finished, catching her off-guard momentarily.

Keisha clicked her light back on, and teased, "You know how to kill the mood."

"But, I did almost die."

"No need to focus on *that*," she said.

"M's my girl," he fumbled, confused with himself.

She gripped his hand and placed her palm to his and let her fingers dance up and down his slowly.

It tickled, but he didn't pull away. He lingered. Before he could say otherwise, she pulled herself close to him—within an inch of his lips. "I wouldn't make you eat lunch by yourself . . . not if you were with me at WKU."

"That's not possible," he said. "College, I mean. I didn't apply, because of the costs and—"

"Then we better treat this special," she added. "Every time we go into Wild Cave could be our last together."

The heat from her body and smell of her perfume were intoxicating. Cade looked at the cave's edge and heard Amelia snickering at Quinn's stale jokes. He didn't see, or hear, M and King.

He instinctively reached down and wiped his sweaty palms on his jeans, felt the paper map inside his pocket. "I have a girlfr—"

"I know," she said. "She's right over there." Keisha pointed, her exotic glow evident even in the poorly lit cave. Her skin was smoother than anything Cade had ever brushed against. Her legs bumped against his where they sat. She leaned in so close her lips were practically on top of his, and he didn't think he could stop—when he heard faint splashing sounds and a high-pitched Amelia shouting, "Get her!" But, Amelia's words were muffled by the cave's echoes.

He let go of Keisha and ran around the corner. Instinctively, he pushed the light to its highest setting. It penetrated the murky water only slightly. Cade looked from Quinn to King—who now stood resolute beside Leslie—and eventually landed on Amelia. "What's happening?!" he shouted. "Where's M?!"

Amelia's shaky finger pointed out into the Echo, and she said, "She's out there. She just fell . . ."

"What? You're sure he didn't push her?!" he screamed, pointing at King.

"She just went under," Amelia said, her voice haunted, distant.

Cade didn't wait for anyone. His fears were pushed into the deepest recesses of his head. *How could I be so stupid?* He flung his helmet off, ripped out of his clothes, and dove into the water. Simultaneously, Quinn removed his helmet, too.

"If Cade goes under—," King started, "I will close this entire cave down," his voice stone cold, and his eyes on Cade's gear, his abandoned clothes.

"He can't swim that good. We *know*. But, give him a sec," Quinn said.

The group waited, as Cade dove under again and again. He went out into the water to the depths where he could no longer touch, and he felt the almost freezing temperature penetrate his toes. His lungs burned, and he could've sworn he felt camp shrimp and fish at his heel. *What if I can't find her? What if I lose her forever like Dad?* His mind reeled, and his gasps echoed against the cave walls. Cade dove under and remained under as long as he could. Then, just as suddenly, he felt a hand grab his—at the bottom of the pit. He pushed with his legs as hard as he could from the pool's tenebrous bottom, and the hand, and body, came with him to the surface. M was gasping for breath like he was. Cade guided them awkwardly to the shallower, black water, and eventually stood dripping in front of the party.

Neither spoke.

Quinn said, "Get her a towel!" Leslie fished for a beach towel inside her bag.

"She can have my change of clothes," Amelia offered. "I came prepared after last time."

Keisha looked horrified and couldn't make eye contact with Cade or Mercedes. She said, "I'll be over here," uncertainly, as she sat on a stone.

Mercedes dried off with Amelia's and Leslie's help, and King bulldogged Cade over to the side saying, "What's going on, Rainy? I was talking to Ms. McCall, and she just disappeared into the Echo! Can you explain that? Does it make any sense?"

"And you don't want to admit you pushed her? The nerve!" Cade roared. He shook with rage. He slowly looked at M and she stared at the ground. No matter what he said or did, M wouldn't look up. His girlfriend since forever (and best friend), and he'd left her by herself while he flirted, or whatever he was doing. Cade pulled the dry clothes painstakingly onto his wet, shivering skin.

Keisha still sat alone, not speaking with anyone. Leslie finally stepped over and asked her how she was. She waved her friend away, but Leslie wouldn't go. The two huddled together.

Amelia said, "She's breathing at least. No CPR this time."

Quinn nudged her. "Not funny."

"What? Cade was blue in the face last trip."

"Not helping," Quinn continued. "Let's just walk over here." Quinn led her toward her friends.

Joshua King held his hand out for Mercedes, and she took it. "Let's rest a bit, and when you feel ready, we can keep moving."

She shook her head. "I'm ready now," her voice even, absent of body almost. "And he didn't push me," she said flatly, to Cade. "I lost my balance and fell in."

Cade tried to grab her hand, but she withdrew; she intentionally stared at King instead.

"I'm ready," she said again. "Let's just go back to the surface."

King took her hand and helped her with her pack. Once it was re-strapped, he said, "Cade, you and Quinsey better take point. We'll bring up the rear. Go steady and don't try to leave us," his tone stern. "I have what I want now."

Cade said, "M, I don't want to—"

She turned and walked away. When he tried to follow, King stepped in front of him. "Our lights are only good for so long. Keep moving."

Cade didn't care about their lights. Let it get dark! He welcomed it at this point. Keisha was a brief pipedream, and M almost disappeared like his dad. "M, I—"

"Rainy. You heard me. You can talk later," King said. "Quinn, help him get us home."

And Quinn came alongside his best friend and steered him slowly, awkwardly toward the front of the group. With Amelia, Keisha, and Leslie filing back into line, the expedition was on again. But, all of the excitement and adventure were long gone.

Cade followed Quinn's boots and didn't try to answer any of his friend's nagging questions. Even Quinn was quieter than normal, and he didn't try to turn everything into a joke. The scariest part for Cade, as he belly crawled around cave fissures into the final passages like the giant earthworm he imagined himself to be, was the absence of M's excitement. Her adventurous spirit was dialed down to zero, and she didn't speak once. The enclosed, crawling holes were torturous, and he couldn't breathe. Cade gasped for air along the final series of tunnels—a panic attack hitting him square in the chest. With the walls so close, Quinn couldn't turn and talk him through it. Cade focused on Quinn's squirming motions, his burrowing. The panic attacks lessened, as he felt the cave's tiny spaces gradually expand to a foot, a foot and a half, and finally enough room to crouch and stand again.

When Quinn stood, Cade did likewise, and he turned as quickly as he could to see M's eyes dodging his. She stared at the pebbles on the ground, and King had his hand on her shoulder. Cade walked toward them, but Quinn spun him back. "She's not feelin' it, man. You can see that, can't you?"

The truth was he couldn't. He felt blind. Abandoned. Keisha wasn't looking his way either.

The tired, emotionally threadbare clan exited the cave, and Mercedes walked toward her car automatically.

"Now what?" Cade demanded.

Quinn shrugged his shoulders. "We walk up there and drop this gear off and . . ."

"Brilliant plan, Bates. I love it!" Cade said sarcastically, trudging past his friend into the sunlight. He tried with all his strength to not look in Mercedes' direction again. *Would she ever come back?* Cade entered the cabin, snatched his dad's journal from the top bunk, and walked away from civilization.

***

Finding a nice place to rest along what his spelunker booklet indicated was the Heritage Trail, Cade plopped onto the sunburnt grass and angrily flipped the journal open to a random page and tried to read. Having no luck, eventually the journal fell shut. Cade guarded his eyes against the sunshine. The dry, itchy grass scratched against his back, and his denim jeans clung to his legs. *Dad forgave King. Why can't I?* The realization forced him to swallow painfully, as he was dehydrated. The notion caused him to sit upright too quickly, and his head spun from the Kentucky humidity. He felt his jean pocket for the map, and it wasn't there. He reached inside, and his pocket was completely empty. *That lying fool!* He tossed the booklet across the field, snapped the elastic band over his journal, and held it to his breast. *At least I know what really went down.* He wiped sweat from his eyes and looked at the Heritage Trail. *I'll make sure you never find what you're looking for, liar.*

# CHAPTER TWENTY-NINE

The Heritage Trail intersected another, and Cade didn't see the sign, but discovered where he was soon enough—the cemetery. It was the Old Guides' Cemetery Trail, and the ancient tombstones stood eerily among the cave trails. Like a monument signifying relics from the past, the cemetery stood in stark contrast to the manicured trails for paying cavers. The Cemetery Trail revealed stones marking guides—their legacies notched onto the limestone tablets. Much like the labyrinthine limestone below the earth's surface, these headstones were marked with the same type of stone. Cade shuddered as he read names completely foreign to him.

He heard her before he saw her, reading, "STEPHEN BISHOP, FIRST GUIDE & EXPLORER OF THE MAMMOTH CAVE. DIED JUNE 15, 1859 IN HIS 37TH YEAR." It was the man he'd read so much about, and it was M's voice. His knees grew weak, and he saw her looking blankly at him. Her green eyes searched his for some semblance of hope.

"This is the guy I told you about, M," he said, unsure if she'd react at all.

She looked back to the tombstone. "What about him?"

"He found the Bottomless Pit."

"So, does that make him a hero or something?"

He took a risk and reached for her hand. "I don't know what I was thinking . . ." he said. "Honestly I don't. And there's something I need to tell you about King. He—"

She yanked away from him, but not viciously. She reached and touched the faded tombstone.

"King stole something from me . . . and Dad. He took a map from my jeans . . . when I went into the water after you. He's a liar, M."

Mercedes turned to Cade and let him look her over. He tried to not blink, afraid she might disappear like an apparition. When he didn't think he could hold his eyes open longer, she gave a frown. "King – a thief? That's a serious accusation."

"It's in Dad's journal. King's been here all these years. King left Dad in a pit, because of something Dad found, but he wouldn't tell King where. Now, King's got Dad's map."

Cade wrapped her up in his arms. He thought of the first time they ventured into the cave at home. Then, he thought of his mom picking blackberries and making cobbler before he left.

M pulled away. "You left me in that cave and . . . and went after her." Tears forming. "If King really did this, and stole that map when I fell, then, this might be life or death."

"I chose *wrong*," he told her. "I didn't do right by you, and—"

"It's not about me right now. It's about getting us out of here alive and—"

"When you went into that water, I didn't care if I drowned, M," he cried.

"We gotta figure out how to get away from here . . . from King. Are you listening, Cade?"

The summer sun continued to make his head spin. The gravestones were sun-bleached and prominent. He saw one with a faded name, and beside the name, the simple descriptor of "Guide" beside it.

As they embraced, the cool, river water dried slowly on their bodies, despite the hundred-degree heat. Cade heard people laughing and kayaking in the distance on the Nolin and Green Rivers.

Cade remembered the divers going after his dad at Spoonbill Dam, returning empty-handed, except for his gear. Mercedes gripped his hand, tugged. Her eyes searched his.

Cade thought of King, and how he'd snooped when he thought M was dying, everyone distracted. King didn't care about anyone but himself. Cade picked up the journal and showed her Haven's entry in '82—about loving his mom forever.

"I feel the same way," she said. "About you, dummy."

Cade looked around the Old Guides' Cemetery lot and admired the peacefulness. He held Mercedes' hand and motioned back up the trail toward the Visitor Center, fairly certain King was already on his way to his destination—to the X on his dad's map.

# CHAPTER THIRTY

Joshua King stood with arms folded, one knee bent and boot resting flush against the Visitor Center wall. He held a cigarette in his calloused fingers and motioned for Cade to come join him.

"You don't have to," Mercedes whispered by his side.

"No, M. I do."

She tugged on his hand and indicated her vehicle – their only escape.

"I know," Cade added, breaking her grip and walking up the trail slowly.

King flicked the cigarette into the freshly mown grass and pushed himself away from the wall. He stood taller than Cade, and his boots were dirty from earlier. He retrieved the already tattered map from his shirt pocket and beckoned Cade closer. "I need you to enlighten me of something, Mr. Rainy ... before you leave, of course."

"I figured you'd already have it figured out. You have the map," he said, inching closer. "You have Dad's markings."

"I do. But, your dad was quite a sneak. See how he cryptically drew it? It looks like Wild Cave is the route, but he writes stuff I can't quite make out ... abbreviations and whatnot. I'm gonna need you to decipher it, or—"

"Forget it!" Cade snapped. "I'm not doing anything else for you."

King leaned into Cade's personal space—their noses almost touching. "I wasn't asking," he said, tired, red-rimmed eyes staring. His calloused right hand reached around Cade's neck, before he could turn to run, and clamped hard onto his skin.

"Let him go!" Mercedes cried, now standing at her open, driver side door.

"Doesn't concern you," he said, over his shoulder. "Doesn't concern anyone here except Rainy. Right, Cade?"

Cade tried to shake himself loose, but he wasn't strong enough. King was too determined. Their eyes were still locked as Cade tried to free himself again.

"Find Daddy's treasure and then you can go back to Seton, got it? Easy peezy."

*If he had been best friends with Dad, their spat over Mom had only been the tip of the iceberg.* Here was a map King was shaking at him, and it was their only ticket out of Mammoth. He didn't want to think about the other ticket out – it wasn't pretty.

King let up on his grip, and Cade got his arm free. Mercedes got out of her car, closed the door and walked back toward her boyfriend slowly.

"I didn't know you smoked," Cade deflected.

"That's what you want to talk about?" King laughed. "Boy, you are dimwitted."

"You have our attention, Joshua," Mercedes interrupted. "Okay?"

"M, go get help," Cade said, staring at King. "Do it. Now!"

"I'm not leaving you. I—"

"You're right," King said. "You're not. No one is. There's no need to get ugly, Rainy. Honestly. This is just a matter we need to resolve and then you're free to go *home.*"

"Amelia and the others—"

"Aren't gonna do anything, because we aren't going to bother them. They're at dinner, and I'd prefer to not take this further than I have to. Besides, she's my niece. Who's she gonna side with you think?"

*Quinn! He's my only chance,* Cade thought.

"Don't get so jittery," King interrupted. "Going crazy won't do you or anyone else a bit of good. And once I have your help . . . You're free." He smiled hideously.

"You won't get away with this!"

"I already have," King replied, scratching his beard. "We're cave guides. And that's what we're doing here. Nothing else. You show me what these scribbles on the map mean, where this treasure is, and we're done. What did Haven mean when he wrote this notation?"

Cade shakily peered at the map, as King slapped it against the side of the Visitor Center wall – holding Cade's neck with his other hand. "Look at it, boy!" his voice almost a coughing wheeze.

There were noises inside the center and distant footsteps, too.

"Sometime today," he barked, looking around.

"Someone is gonna see us!" Cade pleaded.

"And then what?"

Cade thought of Quinn. *If he would just stop flirting for a few minutes and come outside.*

As if reading his mind, King said, "He's not man enough to do anything, Rainy. Besides, my niece is all that's on his mind." He laughed. "So, look at the map and spill." His hand forcefully turning Cade's head back to the map one more time.

There were obvious markings where his dad had designated Gorin's Dome and other landmarks. King should know that already, he thought. But, Cade looked where the markings were, and King kept stabbing at the map with his finger. He saw abbreviations and recognized them almost at once. *Of course!* His poker face must've showed too quickly, because King tightened his already firm grip. "Tell me where the treasure is, boy!"

The abbreviations were exactly like the ones his dad made when he'd been a coal miner. They were dynamite suggestions for clearing rock. *It was a treasure map for precious stones!* It wasn't a simple "grab and go" job, but it was a thorough explosives job. Cade imagined his dad discovering the edges of gemstones and stowing the notes away on a map. *An Adventure he'd wanted to share.* It wasn't meant for greed and profit. He knew that's what King wanted though. *That's why Dad hid it all along!*

"It's not for you!" Cade barked suddenly and tried to pull away—offering no answer.

King fought him and forced him to look at the map again.

Cade laughed and caught King by surprise.

Mercedes inched closer to the Visitor Center door, trying to get inside.

"Stay put, little missy," King scolded.

Cade looked over King's opposite shoulder and saw Quinn creeping around the edge of the center's wall. He was wiping what looked to be sloppy joe from his lip. Then, his friend placed his finger to his lips.

Cade inhaled sharply, and King snapped his head in the direction of the teen's eyes, but not before Quinn lunged forward and speared King's midsection. The impact drove the man and his map backward into the building's wall with a tremendous *thunk* – King knocking his head hard against the cinder blocks. He fell and landed with a harsh thud. The map fell across his eyes, and he tried to grasp for any part of Quinn he could find.

"Leave him alone, King," Quinn barked. "What's your problem?"

"Let's get out of here!" M shouted, cranking the engine, bringing her vehicle to life.

Cade took off in her direction.

"I'll be fine," Quinn said, landing another hit on King with the map still strewn across his face.

"You're leaving with us, Quinn!"

"I'm giving you a head start. Go!"

"I'm keeping you alive," Cade countered, racing back and prying him away from a writhing King whose lip was now bleeding, his mouth spewing profanities.

King started to sit up, disoriented. "I know where you live, Rainy. You aren't going anywhere I don't know like the back of my hand. I'll get my treasure, if it costs me everything. I know where Mommy lives, too."

"I'll rip you apart if you even say her name," Cade said across the grassy lawn.

Quinn pulled him toward Mercedes' ride, and they got in. King wiped his lip and picked the map up from the ground. By this time, Amelia and several others were taking in the scene and asking King if he was all right. He waved them away, but he pointed at the trio leaving. "It's fine." He fake laughed. "I was reminding Cade he's always welcome back anytime he pleases. No need to run away."

Amelia helped her uncle inside the Visitor Center, glaring at Quinn the entire way. Keisha looked at Cade and started to wave, but saw Mercedes and put her hand down. Cade watched the state park recede into the distance as M drove and Quinn kept stammering on and on about how he'd hit Joshua King like a linebacker. He wanted to know what was really up. It was odd and exhilarating, Cade knew, and Quinn didn't know what he'd just done.

"We stood up for Dad," Cade said flatly, as his two friends stared at him. "We kept his treasure safe . . . at least for a little while."

# CHAPTER THIRTY-ONE

Abbott Mize scolded Clay, his gelding, and demanded he walk along the fence line slowly. Clay resisted and fought the aging man step by step. Hollie laughed at the two as she brought clothes in from the line. When she emerged in the kitchen, she handed the basket to Mercedes, asking her if she'd start folding laundry.

Cade said, "Why'd you get rid of the dryer, Mom? All these years, and you decide to move backward in technology. It'd be a lot easier if you just bought a new one."

"Sure it'd be easier." She grinned. "But, I wouldn't get to watch Mize wrestle with that gelding, and I can't miss that."

Mercedes smiled likewise and said, "It is pretty funny, Cade. You gotta admit."

He leaned in and kissed his wife. The two hovered, until Hollie said, "Get a room."

Cade laughed and didn't try to hold it in. His mom's humor—much like Abbott's—made him glad they'd returned to Seton. The foothills beyond Cobank Mountain were some of the prettiest in all the country. He didn't want to move somewhere else, just because he could. Quinn had sure tried to get him out of the hills. Now, Cade heard Quinn was living in St. Louis or somewhere in Missouri. He couldn't fathom spending a week, let alone a lifetime, in a city as big as that. Millions of people milling about trying to get somewhere faster than they needed to. It unnerved him. Abbott's attempts to get somewhere with his horse were entertaining enough.

Mercedes said, "Hollie, do you think we should name the baby Haven, if it's a boy? Cade already thinks it's a boy."

Hollie folded pieces of linen and refolded bedsheets in the stack. She looked up and smiled at the mention of a new life. "Haven's a fine name, but I'm biased, of course. It's your baby. I'll love it even if it was born with scales on its back."

"Mom, what a thing to say!"

"Well, I mean it. No name could make me love it less."

"What about Joshua? Would Joshua make you mad?" Cade heard himself ask.

Hollie held her breath, slowly exhaling. "Of course not. That's a good strong name from the Bible. I like it just fine," she said, adding, "regardless of what else comes to mind."

"Mom. I know Dad forgave him, even though he didn't deserve it."

Hollie stared at her son. "You don't know what you're sayin' Cade," she said flatly.

Cade retrieved the wadded journal entries. Hollie's eyebrows rose up, and the creases in her face became taut. "Where did you . . . Why are you just now showing me these? This is why I was nervous about you going to Mammoth Cave in the first place."

"Maybe we should talk about something else. Wanna feel the baby kick?" Mercedes asked.

Hollie stared at the journal entries, the penmanship she knew so well, and then reached for them. "Let me see it, Cade."

Cade moved backward and Hollie advanced; her grin reappearing.

"What do you want to see an old thing like this for anyway?" he asked.

"They were Haven's notes *to me*," her voice said, growing tiny. "He claimed he lost them at Mammoth. I guess Joshua had these all along?" she said.

He reached outward to her, and she clutched the wad of journal pages tightly. "What's he say?"

"The last one should tie up some loose ends."

She found the dog-eared page. Her eyes filled with tears, and he couldn't remember the last time he'd seen her so unguarded. Hollie covered her mouth. "He did forgive him, didn't he?"

"Of course. That was Dad," Cade said. "Always forgiving. And . . . look at the words at the bottom."

Her eyes leapt to what he'd written and she laughed. Eventually, she handed the pages back, and said, "I forgive Joshua, too. No matter what he's done."

"Just like that? What if King comes here and tries to cause trouble again?"

"Why should I remain angry with someone who lives for so little? It doesn't make sense. No. I forgive him, and I'd speak to him if I ever saw him again. He was a friend before he was anything else," she added.

Cade folded the pages. "Do you even know what you're saying?"

Hollie covered her mouth.

"Don't, Cade," Mercedes mumbled.

"King didn't deserve Dad's forgiveness, and he doesn't deserve yours," he added, and their heads turned to him.

Mercedes deflected, saying, "Mize is a good strong name, don't you think?"

Hollie laughed. She didn't want to argue either. "Of course I forgive him. None of us deserve forgiveness, but we have to give it, or, we'll just die miserable, won't we?"

Cade felt King deserved to be ridiculed, for his sins to be broadcast widely. *His greed.* But, his mom wasn't playing along. Neither was M, as she grabbed his hand and put it against her belly.

"It kicked!" she said.

He knelt and felt Mercedes' growing stomach. *There was life inside!* "M, this is a scary, beautiful blessing. Are you happy?"

Abbott Mize entered the ranch home. "Happy with what?"

Cade stood to his feet. "I was asking the missus, if she was happy with this *Adventure*," he said, pointing to her stomach.

"She better be," Abbott said. "It's hard to turn back now. And no . . . I'm not speaking from experience," their aging neighbor joked.

"What do you think of the name Mize?" Mercedes asked him.

"Well, if it's a him, then I'm for it. But, if it's a her she might get beat up at school. I tend to stay away from them gender neutral ones. Gets confusing. What girl names do you have?" he asked, his work-driven eyes surveying them.

"We haven't made it that far yet."

"Well, you better get cracking, because it's already showing. It might come before you get a name, and no baby deserves a rushed naming. How do you think I ended up with Abbott?" he asked, seriously.

The three stared at his sweat-stained face.

"Well . . . any guesses?"

Mercedes said, "Was it the name of someone in your family?"

"Nope. Worse. It was the name of a cleaning supply in my parent's house and I'm stuck with it. Just like that." He snapped his fingers.

Cade grinned. "Well, Mr. Mize. You seem to be confident enough to tell that story. So, it ain't all bad."

"Now, Cade," he started. "You know I don't like being called Mr. Mize any more than you like being called Cadydid. Am I right?"

"I guess you have a point. So what's going on out there? You gonna just keep beating Clay until he rolls over and finally dies?"

Abbott scratched his scraggly chin. He surmised the field, the gelding. He looked to the tobacco crop growing, much to the credit of Cade's help earlier in the season. "Think we can get that tobacco cut sometime soon? I'd love to get that stuff curing before too long. Do you think we could get to it?"

Cade swallowed a gulp of sweet tea and set the cup down on the table. "Let's start right now. I feel pretty good." He leaned down and kissed M's belly and then Hollie's forehead. "Tobacco won't cut itself."

"No it won't, boy," Abbott said, excited by the news. He followed Cade out to the field.

Cade found the rawhide gloves Abbott once let him use—to dig post holes. He recalled the amount of blood and blisters he'd formed in that first job. He held them up and grinned at the labor they'd endured. "These all right for tobacco?"

"Any glove'll do," Abbott agreed. "But those seem to like you. Now, I'll get the axes, and I want you to get the tobacco sticks. They're over there in the corner of the barn."

Cade retrieved them and brought as many out into the open air as he could carry. He stacked them in a pile, and Abbott said, "That's good for a start. Let's get the plants cut, and then we'll worry about staking them. It's early enough that we should be able to get what we cut off the ground by nightfall. We don't want to leave any to the dew and moisture."

"Roger that, Mize," Cade teased with a mock salute. "Do you think we can keep a little bit for ourselves? You know . . . before it goes to market?"

"Why would we want uncured tobacco?" Abbott spat some juice as he spoke.

"Well, we could cure it ourselves . . ."

"That's a lot of work, you know?" Abbott countered, not unkindly.

"I just thought that since we're growing it, we might as well keep some and try to salvage it ourselves. If it's good, we can package it and call it Mize & Rainy's Blend."

"Like the name," Abbott agreed. "Do you think it'd sell?"

"I think you could sell anything."

"Even bad tobacco?"

"If you had to, I think you could," Cade admitted, and he really meant it.

Abbott said, "Well, the first stack you cut . . . tell you what. You cut it and set it aside. We'll strip it and *try* to cure it on our own. Might get sick as dogs, but it's your idea. If it's bad, we'll just puke, and I'll blame you. How does that sound?"

Cade saw the old man's smile, his creased forehead and sweaty brow. The best mentor he'd had since Spoonbill Dam. He said, "Deal," and Abbott shook his hand.

"Let's cut some Mize & Rainy's Blend," Mize joked and set off with one hatchet.

Cade took the other and spliced the tobacco plants' stalks. He set the first portion aside for their next *Adventure*. It struck him that Abbott was one adventure and Mammoth another. M was his lifelong partner-in-crime, and he was seeing the differences in each. But, the culmination of them together equaled one life, one streaming memory. *It was a blessing to know them . . . to love them.* He thanked God for the family and the friends. He thought about the young boy, or girl, growing inside M's belly, and he chopped the stalks faster. It was an amazing thing how life grew from the inside out. The world was full of life, and he helped add to it every day. Everyone in his family did. Haven did. Hollie did. He looked back to the ranch home and thought he saw M looking out the window.

The smell of tobacco resonated with him, and he chopped all the more feverishly before darkness fell upon the land.

# Acknowledgments

Writing a novel truly takes a God-given village. I'm thankful for so many people this time around. Martin Jones for having the patience of Job in this novel's construction. We made it! Journey Chattanooga for reading and supporting. Kirt Rogers for steering the ship away from all things derivative. Russell Helms for all those Thursday night hang sessions. eLectio Publishing for opening the door and providing the foothold for this book to be a blessing to others. Mammoth Cave National Park (& the National Park Service) for assistance in the research. My grandparents for being such strong examples of family. Nathan Davis for always reading. We've built an entire novel in emails alone throughout the years. Dana Jones for giving this novel a second look and providing invaluable feedback. Cody S. Decker for his friendship and for writing on a typewriter. My best friends: Adam, JT, Dani, and Lindsey for being the stuff of legends. You make storytelling fun. *Bring back the good times!* Thanks to the Bluegrass Writers' Studio, EKU, and MFA alum. Thanks to Cage the Elephant for providing music for all those hours of editing. Bowling Green's finest. Thanks to my beautiful wife, Leah, who married a man with more than a few screws loose. You are a queen and a saint. To God, for being the same yesterday, today, and forever.

## About the Author

**BRIAN L. TUCKER** grew up in the Lake Cumberland region of southern Kentucky. His debut novel, *Wheelman,* was featured on NPR, and promoted in places such as Star Line Books, McKay's of Tennessee, Barnes & Noble, and Amazon. He is currently blogging personal stories and adventures at: BrianLTucker.com.

Made in the USA
Lexington, KY
14 August 2017